GOOD INTENTIONS

DAN SABER

"It is hard to explain the place filled by political concerns in the life of an American… If an American should be reduced to occupying himself with his own affairs, at that moment half his existence would be snatched from him; he would feel it as a vast void…"

 —Alexis de Tocqueville

"The most merciful thing in the world, I think, is the inability of the human mind to correlate all its contents. We live on a placid island of ignorance in the midst of black seas of infinity, and it was not meant that we should voyage far. The sciences, each straining in its own direction, have hitherto harmed us little; but some day the piecing together of dissociated knowledge will open up such terrifying vistas of reality, and of our frightful position therein, that we shall either go mad from the revelation or flee from the light into the peace and safety of a new dark age."

 —H.P. Lovecraft

EPISTLE

I sit alone in a Salt Lake City motel, pondering my eternity between the erratic beeps of the broken microwave. Plush pink chairs and lime green carpet conspire to radiate a judgmental heat. Also, the AC is busted. As I stare at the vending machine Hot Pocket thawing in my hand, I can't help but feel that it's all been a dud.

My name is Zeke, and for eons, I worked at *THOROUGHGOOD1*, humanity's heavenly bureaucratic overseer. As an agent in the Department of Inspirations, my job was to inspire the creative among your kind to make minor works of art. Before you assume anything — before you begin dreaming of tales featuring Van Gogh, Austen, or Dostoevsky — I should reaffirm: *minor*. While my colleague Maribel inspired the cave paintings in Lascaux, I inspired forgettable cooking concepts like *Stone Chef* and *MasterGatherer*. When Diana inspired Hammurabi's Code, I swam in her wake by pumping out lazy true crime like *Eye for an Eye: Extreme Slave Whippings*. Though G. did permit me to inspire a book for his New Testament, when he read my submission, he hurled it from Old World to New. "NO ONE CAN EVER — AND I MEAN *EVER* — FIND THIS," he yelled, but it was later found all the same, by a man named Joseph Smith. I defended my inspiration, shouting, "It was a burlesque! A burlesque!" to anyone who'd listen, but Clara, my old boss, wasn't convinced. She was "finally forced" to split our department in two: Grand Narratives would inspire works of art like *The Great Gatsby*, *Guernica*, and WrestleMania X-Seven. My team — Frivolous Pursuits — would handle the rest.

Thus, on the margins have I toiled.

I rebooted *Chopped (and That's It)*! as a competitive vegan cooking show, inspired album filler for a past-his-prime Eminem, and even made an NBC executive think he'd lost his mind by inspiring him to consider an *Eye for an Eye / Law and Order* crossover, *Law and Order: Whipped in Hammurabi's Court.* When I later relaunched *Eye for Eye* as a YouTube series, I learned that while it was too extreme for Mesopotamia and NBC, it would never be extreme enough for YouTube, whose vicious preteen audience demanded ever more elaborate whippings until YouTube was "finally forced" to suspend my account. I've been nominated for two Adult Film Awards, both for Best Sound Editing (one in the Stepmom Scream category, another in Synchronized Grunt in a Gangbang).

They are my only critical acknowledgments.

I should stop, lest the motel manager return and ask me again to refrain from sobbing. Besides, the point is not to recount an eternity of mediocre inspirations. I know this isn't what you had in mind when you imagined heaven or its hosts. But I'll need you to come to terms with your newfound knowledge quickly. We've got a lot to cover before I can get to my real point: apologizing for my role in your looming apocalypse.

My eternity may have been a dud, but I can at least do this one good thing.

Yours,

Zeke

P.S. I know I lack the proper permits to inspire this project, but I'm claiming an exception under *Standards & Practices 6.2.17: Leveling with Humanity in Event of Apocalypse both (a) Probable and (b) Imminent.* While I'm aware that the last agent to claim a 6.2.17 ended up de-winged — Ned Ludd just couldn't let those damned mechanized looms alone — this time is different: who's left to stop me?

IN THE BEGINNING

THOROUGHGOOD 1

G. realized that humans had free will when they emerged, seemingly overnight, from the gene pool of a tiny, paranoid marsupial named Elvis. But how, G. wondered, would humanity's cobbled together genetics manifest a quality as profound, beautiful, and *mysterious* as free will? The answer was immediate and disappointing: as douchiness. From the start, humans engaged in a litany of unfortunate behavior: destroying other species, organizing backrooms deals with rival deities, and, most discouragingly of all, failing to approach G.'s work with even a semblance of artistic curiosity.

"And so you know why it's wrong to sell your wife?" asked G.

"Well, no," said Adam. "Did you not say I had dominion over her?"

"Jesus, no," said G. anachronistically.

"Then why include that line?"

G. sighed. "I had a feeling that might be too sophisticated. Look, this is probably my fault. First, you shouldn't calibrate your moral compass this way."

"What's a comp —"

"Second," said G., becoming more agitated, "even if you calibrate your moral compass this way, that line doesn't *literally* mean you own anyone. I'm trying to convey the brutal cosmic consequences of your split with a me-type entity. I want to craft a literary universe with some genuine conflict here: the snake's enmity with Eve, her pain in childbirth, your 'dominion' over her. The Adam in the Bible should be raging *against* these consequences of sin — these perversions of

The Almighty Creator's Creation — not embracing them as though they were commands from on high. You understand this, yes?"

The following day, Adam hired a band of marauders. They stormed the Neanderthal village Eve was in and burned it down, making the leader of the village watch as his wives and children vanished in the flames. Snatching Eve out of a burning hut, Adam turned toward the survivors.

"Never cross me again!" he yelled.

They looked at him blankly, fearful and confused.

———————

For millennia, G. hoped a sentient bunch would come along to contemplate his art and internalize his subtle prescriptions for harmonious and enlightened living. You can imagine his disappointment with humanity. Although you occupied the same planet, your worlds didn't resemble his, all texture and vibrancy. You had a compulsion to make sense of your surroundings but not the complete set of cognitive tools; rather than trying to conquer your limitations, you hammered away complexity and excised ambiguity, building dreary monuments to first-order thinking: one cause, one effect. Not exactly something that could be fixed by an art appreciation class.

Despite this, G. considered himself a pro, so shaking off his disappointment, he devised solutions. Humanity had promise, more than the monkey and more, even, than the smarter-but-douchier dolphin. What you needed was *guidance*. To rein in creation, G. realized, he would need to replace his arty, lukewarm dictums with clear-cut commandments. Free will would need to be replaced by total control.

So G. ran it all: every drought and every storm, every birth and death, every marriage and every predetermined divorce. He authored rules and regulations, held posts in every government, and issued a list of animals that could make reasonable pets (which was superfluous, since he also assigned everyone's pets). When a king resigned his post to pursue dance, G. strapped him to the throne. When a girl discontinued her dance lessons to study animal husbandry, G. marched her back into the studio. When an opium addict thought about cleaning up his life, maybe reconnecting with his son and figuring out if his wife would take him back on a trial basis, G. hotboxed him in a room filled with pictures of the clear-skinned man Jeremy called "Daddy" now.

Which… harsh in a *vacuum*, sure. But the king had to be king so the girl could grow up, get entertainment credentials to perform in the royal court, and kill him. The girl's regicidal leanings had to stem from: (1) Her dance instructor, who disliked the king for his frequent feedback on "the theory of dance instruction"; (2) A bribe from the opium addict, who during a royal parade mistook the king for his son's new dad; and (3) Her own frustration at having to dance, especially for a person so annoyingly passionate about it. All of *this*, if you could believe it, was necessary to facilitate the reign of a wonderful queen, who would save her people from famine through judicious resource planning. If G. had simply *installed* the queen, however, she wouldn't have grown up during the incompetent reign of the dance-distracted king, experiencing a number of life events dependent on a complex system of equations whose solutions needed to satisfy not only this constraint but an infinite number of others, all while maximizing the rate of growth in global artistic appreciation.

Thus, hands-on intervention worked — at least for a few millennia. But while such systems can work in the early innings of a new development, they inevitably run into problems scaling. The informal guidelines that work when mediating disputes between two brothers fail on a global scale, but G. tried to apply them in a straightforward, artless way. For instance, when G. punished the instigators of an unapproved minor war by saying they would no longer be able to farm the land (*a la* Cain), they resorted to cannibalism. Moreover, unlike the Cain and Abel days, G. lacked the time (or maybe just the energy) to explain such decisions, the important but hard to parse purposes they served, the intricate ways they built on each other.

This combination of micro-management *sans* one-on-one time resulted in a global malaise: a pervasive, enervating belief that life's certainty robbed it of its meaning. This, in turn, produced a movement revolving around drugs, drink, and fornication, an unstoppable tide that not even G. himself could contain. Human population had grown too large, human dissatisfaction too rampant. Entire cities sank into pits of sexual perversion and alcoholic excess. Government ground to a halt. Farmers converted cropland into drugland. Families gave way to permanent, roving, Borg-like orgies, consuming sons, daughters, and creepy uncles. They ravaged the landscape like tornados, and because the ratio of men to women in these things was more lopsided than that of a Silicon Valley tech office or third-tier fraternity party, when two orgies met, the fight for women was cataclysmic.

G. did keep one family from slipping into Sodom, but not because of any special insight. He'd simply invested more time in his relationship with Noah because Noah and Adam were relatives, and G. found this ancestral link compelling for sentimental reasons (now fully against *Standards*). In fact, it was Noah, not G., who pitched the idea of a Soft Reset (see 7.3.109 of *TG1 Standards & Practices* for more, but briefly: "An Apocalyptic Event, defined as one that annihilates more than 10% of Current Dominant Species. Must satisfy one or more of the following Reset Criteria: manage population; teach a lesson; more promising species on deck.").

"It's over," said Noah, "We're not getting them back."

"I think we can. It's just going to take some work, some give-and-take," said G. "For example, I've been thinking about implementing a 'Casual Friday,' where people can do whatever they want so long as they work hard Saturday to Thursday. That could be fun…"

"I don't think so," said Noah, turning suggestively towards a picture of his family tree, where an empty space remained under Abel's name. "My sons and wives are scared to leave the house. We need to start over."

G. found the idea nauseating. What kind of deity wipes out most of his constituents? I mean, sure, you could look at a pie chart of G.'s inbound sacrifices and correctly point out that Noah's family contributed the majority. And, yes, you could argue that G. wouldn't be wiping out most of humanity *solely* for his primary donor, but because he believed in the idea, somehow: after all, who better to know about the plight of humanity than a human? Still, G. felt guilty.

"No one would trust me after this," he said.

"We still would," said Noah. "Sometimes, leaders need to make tough choices."

G. needed time, so taking on the form of a finch, he left Noah and flew to what's now the site of the Space Needle. He preferred this combination of hemispheres when he wanted to think. It was quieter here, with kinder, more down-to-earth people (which G. knew, because when deciding which humans would live where, he only led his favorites across the land bridge connecting Russia and Canada).

Hopping along the sinewy branch of a cedar, G. looked down at the maze of tents and canoes. The village was quieter than usual. It had been a year since he'd checked in, but he loved the leader he'd installed: a tall and honorable man named Puyallup. Regardless of what was happening elsewhere in the world, here, G. knew, things would be okay.

As the grey clouds melted into a mist, the leaves began to glisten and G.'s avian compatriots engaged him in sing-song chirping. A shout echoed through the trees, prompting G. to peek down, where he saw two boys chasing a girl in a game of tag. He smiled as the children ran through a tent and jumped over a dormant fire pit. He giggled as a mother washing clothes shook her head in the bemused way mothers do. He laughed as the girl ducked behind a tree, covering her eyes to thwart her playmates. He watched as the boys found and tagged her. Felt confused as they shoved her into the base of the tree. Apprehensive as they ripped one of the straps from her dress. Panicked as their laughs went silent and their eyes turned violent.

Before anything else could happen, G. was streaming down the trunk of the tree, his wings morphing into human arms, beak transmuting into a mouth yelling, "Stop! Stop! Stop!" He landed between the boys and the girl, and when it became clear he wouldn't let the game continue, the boys shook their heads and ran off.

The girl stood up, brushed the more noticeable globs of mud from her faded yellow dress, and stared up at G. "What'd you do that for?"

G. turned, paused for a moment, and lifted up his hands. "They were attacking you."

"Yeah, that's the game," she said.

G.'s nausea returned. "They would have hurt you."

"Yeah, *that's the game.*"

G. took three deep breaths, making the trees around him tilt inward and outward in rhythm. Finally, he asked, "Where's Puyallup?"

"Ha! He's been gone for a long time."

"What do you mean? Where did he go?"

"Nowhere," she said, smirking as she pointed at a tent in the center of the village.

G. motioned the girl to stay, but as soon as he turned toward the tent he heard her scamper through some leaves and into a stream. He shook his head, which intensified his headache, and stumbled to the tent. The flaps refused him. Bending down, G. saw a red thread binding the flaps together, so he ripped them apart and stepped into the dark ready for a fight. Instead, he got a smell: a combination of smoke and wet and vomit that made him gag. As his eyes adjusted, a black outline crystallized into a corpse, betraying its minimal life by wheezing, moaning, and dragging a pair of clay figures from model forest to model canoe.

When it registered the disturbance, the corpse looked up, and the pupils of its eyes disappeared. "Uuuu-UUuu-UUUUU-uuuuuUUUuuUu," it said, with at least some awareness of the drama of the moment.

"Puyallup? Is that you?" asked G.

"Was," said Puyallup. "Was."

"What's wrong with you? Do you know what's going on in your village? We need to discuss this *now*."

Puyallup ignored the command. He'd clearly been waiting a long time for G. to return, because he made a gesture of grandiosity toward his lumpy clay figurines and in an uncharacteristically poetic way said, "You made me chief, but I am no chief. I am at heart a toymaker, but you denied my heart."

G. counted down from three once more. "What are you talking about? You could have told me you wanted to be a toymaker."

"Did... You didn't listen..." said Puyallup, coughing as he rolled onto his back.

"We could have worked something out," G. said. "You had the best temperament, is all. And natural strengths — like height, you see. But... but... I've been bouncing around this 'Casual Friday' idea that's received a pretty good reception and might address, you know, some of these issues..."

Moments passed, the stench filling the silence. Puyallup sat up. "I had those strengths when you were here. The threat disappeared, and then I disappeared."

Puyallup's words struck G. as important, so he noted them for later. At the moment, he was having trouble staying focused, because as his eyes adjusted further to the dark of Puyallup's tent, G.'s anger was giving way to a renewed and violent nausea, this one brought on by the army of dead rats that surrounded the growth of fluorescent orange mushrooms at Puyallup's feet.

"So you're saying," G. said, trying to avoid Puyallup's wild, diverging irises, "that you needed encouragement. A level of motivation I wasn't providing you. *That's* the main problem, yes?"

Puyallup turned back to his toys and gave each figurine a miniature wooden fishing rod. He crawled to the other side of his tent and pulled open the door of an oven, producing a clay fish from within. Puyallup returned to his toys and tenderly placed the fish in the canoe. With his pupils returning, Puyallup looked at the scene and sighed. He clapped twice, commenting aloud that one of the fishermen had caught the fish and was now bragging to his companion. Satisfied with the scene, Puyallup grabbed a mushroom, popped it in his mouth, and died.

———

Now this had all been some dark shit.

However, as G. is fond of saying: "A light shineth in the darkness, and the darkness comprehended it not." Or to put it in plainer terms: Puyallup gave G. an idea. Maybe Noah was right. Perhaps a Soft Reset *was* a good idea, not because he thought it necessary, but because the very *threat* of a Soft Reset might render the follow-through unnecessary. If humans wanted to avoid oblivion, then they would need to embrace G.'s decisions, or at least accept them without joining roving orgies or overdosing on mushrooms. Perhaps looming annihilation plus Casual Fridays would fix everything.

"This is a great idea," said Noah.

"You think so?" asked G.

"Absolutely. 100% brilliant and foolproof. This is why you're in charge and we are but humble, you know, bees in your cosmic hive."

G. was feeling confident, proud even.

"Of course," Noah said, "you'll need to put on a convincing show. People need to think you'd follow through. Not saying you'll have to follow through — I mean, it's a dynamite plan — but the threat of destruction needs to be *palpable*."

"Of course," said G., reclining on Noah's couch, "of course."

Coming up with the right existential threat proved harder than G. anticipated. Earthquakes seemed too sudden, meteors too clichéd. A famine felt too prolonged, while no one would be able to focus on righteousness during a drought. Volcanic eruptions felt more promising, but when humans inevitably returned to the Lord's flock he wanted the apocalyptic process to be reversible, and volcanoes were finicky. G.'s brainstorming sessions were sapping him of his initial high when it struck, the sort of divine insight that only comes to people and deities who are on the right path: a global rain that would turn into a global flood.

Here, anyone would agree, was an innovation that met all possible success criteria. The rain would serve as a constant, palpable reminder of doom. It would give humanity a fixed amount of time to get its act together. It would do only minor long-term damage to the earth. It was perfect.

G. informed the leaders he'd installed around the world of the forthcoming destruction. Of the ones who hadn't also overdosed or turned into hermits, the response was positive. Clearly, G. thought, the capable ones had been thirsting for such a solution.

When he was sure everyone had been informed, G. called in his destructive agents. In one part of the world the storm clouds spelled "REPENT" and in another they spelled "RETURN TO ME." In another, more contentious part of the world they spelled "LOOK BOZO, THIS IS YOUR OWN DOING." But in every part of the world they brought rain. And rain. And rain. Sometimes lightning, when G. was feeling saucy, but you could tell the emphasis, the craftsman's focus, was on the dark, uninterrupted streams of big wet drops pooling in city streets and farmland, reminding humanity — with each soggy sandal strap and muddy hemline — of the end's nigh-ness.

And yet, the rain did not elicit G.'s anticipated response. The flood was allowing humans to abdicate responsibility for the ultimate decision. They had all wanted to end things for some time now, but most couldn't bear to do it because the thought of not existing while other people continued to exist was more horrifying than a listless life of heavy petting and dry mouth. Now their perfect storm had come along. A global act of synchronous destruction. A not-so-natural disaster that would eliminate your life but more importantly eliminate the lives of your exes, more attractive siblings, and that college classmate you invited to your wedding but who didn't return the favor.

Humanity was actually relieved.

Meanwhile, on the ark Noah had built ("just in case we needed it"):

Head bent and eyes focused on the deck, G. paced, dodging scampering koalas and confused giraffes. Noah's son Shem herded the escaped great-grandchildren of the original mice back into the rodent quarters, which had devolved into a mess of half-eaten children and intergenerational, cannibalistic turd pullets. Noah's other sons, Ham and Japheth, watched in horrified silence as their favorite animal, a rhino named Charlie, drowned after trying and failing to gore a flamingo after the flamingo struck what rhinos evidently consider to be an inflammatory pose. It was hard to tell the time of day, as sounds blended into one other, the cock crowing becoming the dog barking becoming the lion roaring becoming the cat screeching becoming the cock crowing. (And also because of the rainstorm.)

G. reached the gold-trimmed marble staircase to the captain's quarters Noah had built just in case, sidestepping a crow pecking a spider monkey carcass on his way up.

"This isn't going like I planned," said G. as he entered.

"Yeah, we should've built a separate ark for the animals," said Noah, reclining in the captain's chair, "but you know: live and learn. Wine?"

"That's not what I mean. It's been raining for a week, but no one's repenting. No one's returning. This is a disaster."

"Wasn't that the point?"

G. turned around and opened the door, but before he could leave Noah hopped up from his chair, ran across the room, and put a hand on G.'s shoulder: "Whoa, wait! I'm sorry! Look, I know you're disappointed. I shouldn't have made the comment. But this was the plan. This was always the risk."

"I can't go through with it. I'm calling it off."

"You can't do that, G. If you do, no one will ever believe in your word again. You get one shot at things like this."

G. leaned on the cabin door and slid his behind onto the shimmering maple floor. "I can't."

"You can. Look, you need to start thinking long-term. Sure, you failed with this batch. But let's say you gave them a second chance. What would change? Nothing. They would go right back to their drugs. Right back to their sex. It would be nothing but trouble from here to eternity. But if you finish the job — no, look at me, G. — if you finish the job, painful as it may be, it sends a *permanent* message. That your will is not to be disobeyed. I don't want to be dramatic, but this is make-or-break, G."

G. opened his mouth to argue, but couldn't.

"Look," said Noah, "I understand. You rest, and I'll take care of things from here."

Months passed. The rain ended. Noah and his sons opened the ark, released the surviving animals, and took in the scene.

"My G...." said Japheth.

"It's — it's awful," said Ham.

"There's so many," said Shem.

And there were. Blue, bloated bodies sprouted from the soggy field, picked-at eyes and genitals betraying their recent tenure as fish food. The ones who chose a faster death swung from branches. Others lay emaciated on makeshift rafts, having thought they could wait out the flood — often, it seemed, in the same sinful state that had caused it, their petrified corpses frozen mid-thrust, snort, or swallow.

Rubbing his temples, Noah looked at his sons. "Well, let's get started."

The four embarked on a multi-month cleanup, burning bodies and debris. They also built the infrastructure for a multigenerational conspiracy, one that would ensure future members of humanity believed the contents of G.'s Bible actually happened. The plan was so ambitious, so intricate, so error-prone, so unbelievable that it would take pages and pages of primary sources and argument to prove that it all happened. But you were all ready to take *Da Vinci Code* at its word so I don't feel the need. Noah's children, grandchildren, great-grandchildren, and so on staged mythical Moses's escape from Egypt, planted evidence of diminutive David's run-in with Goliath, sold a guy who happened to be named Joseph into slavery in Egypt. When Noah added in the bit about the flood, he recast G. in a sterner, scarier, and more classically Old Testament light to maintain consistency with the text's grumpy, vengeful deity, who G. himself had fleshed out post-Abel as a metafictional parody of the deity he feared himself becoming. In making the mythical literal, Noah believed he could keep humanity obedient, pliable: the book ceased to be a compendium of G.'s hidden lessons and became instead a heavy-handed warning that destruction was always an angry deity away.

Meanwhile, in heaven, G. sat on his modest throne, devastated. He took no pleasure in the normally pleasurable sight of us soaring. Found no comfort in the normally comforting sensation of the sun's unfiltered rays.

We didn't want to approach him, but after millennia of euphoric, aimless flying, I did.

"G.," I said.

He didn't respond.

"Boss," I said.

Still no response.

"Come on, what's wrong?"

He looked up.

"Can't you see? I've failed."

I looked over my shoulder at my companions, who were motioning me to continue. "We know, boss, but look: some of us have been talking, and we think it's time you get back on the saddle."

G. looked away. "There's not going to be a saddle," he said. "The experiment is over. I'm never going to be that involved again."

"But what about Noah?"

"What Noah did doesn't matter. If anything, he may have helped us."

"How could that be?"

"It gave me an idea."

The idea, of course, was *THOROUGHGOOD1*, a collection of sensible guidelines enforced by angelic administrators, a system of checks and balances on heavenly authority that would prevent similar disasters from recurring. Having seen the consequences of divine mandates, G. willingly ceded his authority. Even with *TG1* approval, he would only influence gently, say, with an unusually effective ad campaign for basketball shoes, or an improbable string of Buffalo Bills Super Bowl losses. He'd tried subtlety and he'd tried control. Now he would try gentle nudges.

But how would G. — or any of us — get approval for such nudges? Permits. Permits would govern everything, from timeline-shifting developments (e.g., superstorms, boy bands) to artistic inspiration. To show you how seriously G. took the new process, I only need point you to his masterwork. Sometime after Noah added the flood story, the Bible picked up a few books on pork and sodomy that were *not* part of the original divine communique. However, to cut them would have required interfering with free will, which as you now know is a big no-no, but could be done — in particularly grievous instances — with a special kind of timeline-resetting permit called a "Hard Reset," or a 9.33, that would actually send humanity back in time to just before the problematic moment happened. But it's been lost in a regulatory labyrinth ever since (along with the one that would have made a certain aspiring artist in Austria better at painting).

G. didn't protest. He applied for a separate permit, this one for permission to send a representative down to earth. This representative would bear a simple message, a rule to supersede all previous rules: *Treat others as you wish to be treated.*

And, well, you know how that turned out.

In other words, if humanity were careening toward an extinction event (usually the case), and repositioning the coordinates of a king/dancer/opium addict/rightful queen quadrangle could save you (sometimes the case), then it was up to G. and *TG1* to produce a permitted plan to effect that repositioning. Admittedly, this has led to some close shaves. During the Bubonic Plague, for example, we tried spreading a public health jingle that went...

> *When you find some buboes there,*
> *On your groin or 'neath your hair,*
> *Don't be scared, but wrap it up*
> *Your time has coooooooome*
>
> *If you can still walk away*
> *Do it before your last day*
> *If you don't, the plague will spread*
> *And cause more deeeeaaaad*

Which, unsurprisingly, failed to *land*, partly because all of our bards died, partly because — in my humble opinion (though nobody asked me) — the song loses momentum halfway through, going from personal and catchy to punch-less and abstract. No one cared about the concept of "more dead," but they might have cared about a neighbor or priest or coworker. Even if they *had* cared, our point was muddled: we said they should leave "before their last day" but should have specified that they leave immediately. Without that sense of urgency, plague victims continued to hang around their families, waiting for death and quickening humanity's downward spiral towards a state grimmer than any time since Genghis Khan vigorously defended himself against a class-action paternity suit.

Luckily, the tune to the song came in handy for *Pinocchio*, and humanity survived.

PART 1:

Heaven

DISRUPTED

THOROUGHGOOD1 headquarters was less a building, really, than a gigantic hollow layer cake orbiting the Milky Way Galaxy. G. built our corporate capitol from shimmering, translucent pink icedust, the same medium he used for the universe's only popular art installation, *Rings of Saturn*. But while *Rings* had an entire planet to keep it in formation, our HQ needed to be its own source of gravity. This resulted in a building so big, so comically impractical that we had to sell all but ten of its 75,000 layers to the universe's other lifeforms, who liked the prestige of owning a floor of Goodville they were simply too busy to use, as well as the opportunities for timeshare development. *Come vacation in the last authentically undeveloped corner of existence!* they'd say in their respective tongues; then, in the universal language of annoying grammar snobs, they'd continue: *A very unique experience… and with "such quaint" natives!*

Sometimes during orbit, when the luminous echo of 200 billion stars stirring 100 billion planets hit the facade *just so*, the building would glimmer as it moonwalked through flickering shades of lavender and orange, grape and maroon. Even the lifeforms without eyes would have told you it was beautiful (minus the Slivgons, who also lacked mouths). Semi-transparency, however, was not without its awkwardness, in that you could see what was happening above and beneath you: the pink-tinged bald spot of somebody using the bathroom one layer down; the slightly more opaque ass of somebody using the bathroom two layers up; the barely discernible pink impression of multi-headed Slivgonic genitalia, individual heads contracting and expanding like Redwood-sized earthworms, relieving themselves by expelling steaming orange slime all over the top-layer gym shower.

(We felt this conception of heaven would be too challenging for you to accept, which is why we emphasized clouds and pearly gates whenever we inspired your artists to depict it.)

Zipping up my fly, I left Goodville by leaping from the Department of Inspirations' bathroom window on the 37,338th floor. The Galaxy's blue and white spirals always popped when emerging from Goodville's pink filter, so I paused, enjoying my view until I could procrastinate no more. I was flying to Cloud Hall, a massive crystal amphitheater that orbited Goodville and looked like a fancy punch bowl (if that punch bowl were hurtling through space). The Hall's name came from its cloud-formed benches, stage, and podium, which — while not practical — did look dynamic and beautiful swirling against the Hall's walls, themselves towering artist achievements bearing frescoes of famous agents:

There was Tyler Z., Head of Permits, rejecting G.'s first permit application for being "Retaliatory." (On the form, you could read the words, "send a swarm of locusts unto Noah's descendants, who are at this moment trying to stuff a guy named Jonah into a whale.")

There was Bruce G., Head of Research, discovering the Bubonic Plague was being spread by rats (meaning we could save humanity by adapting our plague jingle to less discriminating murine audiences).

There was Jimmy D., Head of Political Corrections, who in a tri-paneled fresco was signing the Hard Reset paperwork following the original apocalyptic conclusions to the Spanish Flu, the Cuban Missile Crisis, and the first of Beyoncé's surprise album releases.

There was Clara T., my old boss and former Head of Inspirations, celebrating our first and only Best Picture Award (for *Crash*), and there she was again, a few panels over, being relieved of her duties following the backlash to the movie.

Finally, there was me, stirring G. from his millennia-long depression.

———————

As I flew, Diana and Maribel, my colleagues from Inspirations, joined me. Diana had just completed a six-month assignment in Washington, D.C., where she'd been studying the impact of a new political thriller she'd inspired. The premise of *Filibuster!* was simple: White Cheeks, a super PAC run by Big Sunscreen, has for years been trying and failing to make sunscreen a daily part of America's beauty regimen. Realizing they've hit a wall, White Cheeks hires an ambitious junior Senator named Sonny Sunderson, who in the pilot episode embarks on an infinite filibuster, hoping to stymie all new legislation and, in so doing, facilitate the rise of global warming — or, as White Cheeks would have it, the era of subsidized sunscreen. The rest of Congress must respond to this post-filibuster world, leading to conflict, hilarity, and hallucinogenic ruminations by the Coppertone Girl and her pervert terrier on the role of government in a world that's become too hot to handle. Unfortunately, the show's second season was already in jeopardy. The writer Diana had been inspiring suffered a nervous breakdown shortly after Diana streamed the idea for the finale into him. Of course, she could always inspire someone else, but because creators tend to add their own spin to inspirational streams, Diana worried about compromising the show's tonal universe (which would only get darker anyway).

We were gathering for the bi-annual planning and review session, where the top three of each department met to discuss the results of the preceding semi-fiscal and plan out the next. (While I could hardly be considered the "top" of my department, I was the only agent who specialized in Frivolous Pursuits, so I got the designation by default.) In the past, each department crafted independent plans to carry out G.'s major themes, but recently, for reasons I wish I could explain, the meeting had become political.

Indeed, it had become a time when lurking interdepartmental squabbles de-lurked and occasionally exploded, embroiling other departments in a battle for influence, resources, and G.'s literal blessing. Last meeting, for example, Animal Relations filed a formal complaint against Technological Innovations. The complaint maintained that DTI infringed on DAR territory by launching a number of dating sites under the DODGE-A-BREEDER corporate umbrella, which encouraged dog owners to meet, double date, and in the best case get married and have puppies and in the worst case just have puppies — likewise for cat owners and horse owners, the last of which got weird and litigious due to unclear marketing copy, e.g., "Your horse is a *huge* part of your life, so why not embark on your next journey for love together?"

DTI filed a countermotion, arguing they were unambiguously aiding *TG1's* primary aim of... *What was it again? Ah, yes, connecting human beings.* DAR countered, arguing they'd been empowering animals to make their own decisions in life and in love for a *number* of semi-fiscals, and even if *that* didn't make into last semi-fiscal's executive summary, maybe *someone* could read the whole damned memo for once. With the room dozing off, they also explained how humanity's psychological obsession with breed purity had led to health defects among many dog and cat breeds, and that DODGE-A-BREEDER would exacerbate this by making it easier for, say, French Bulldog owners to meet other French Bulldog owners, thereby keeping the Frenchie gene pool susceptible to some terrifying strain of Francophobic flu. *Plus,* DAR continued, mistaking the room's silence for the reluctant goose-pimpled acceptance of The True, *there was the much — much, much, much — more profound issue of whether your Frenchie's sexual and emotional needs were best met by the kind of conservative relationship that would necessarily emerge from a product that so thoroughly reinforced established notions of canine hierarchy.*

Allow us to clarify, DTI said, *that we have no horse in any of these ethical races. The Total Addressable Market of disrupting purebred breeders is simply more compelling than doing the same for mutts.*

DAR, taken aback by DTI's crass calculus, stumbled over their rebuttal, giving our accountant Larry an opening. He climbed onto the cloud stage, tapped the cloud microphone, and pointed out that DODGE-A-BREEDER had already gone out of business.

In a climate such as this, despite *Filibuster!*'s obvious promise, Diana wasn't optimistic.

"I'm not optimistic," said Diana, "the reaction so far has been the usual Beltway bullshit. Oh no, oh G., I'm even talking like them now."

"Shhh. Time. Takes time," said Maribel, discharging her primary managerial duty of talking Diana back from a ledge. "Do we know how popular the show is?"

"To be honest, I don't know. Research won't get back to me even though I've filed, like, four requests for information. I'll be paying those dweebs an in-person visit soon. But empirically, I went to Off the Record after it premiered and it was all anyone was talking about. It's just not having the intended effect."

"How do you know?" said Maribel. "You can't see what it's in their hearts."

"Well…"

"Diana, you didn't."

"I *had* to. I needed to see if the show was having an effect I couldn't observe directly."

"You can't snoop without a permit."

"Come on, Maribel, I was in and out. Frankly, reading the thoughts of those D.C. cretins was darker than anything I inspired McKarren to write for the show. I should be the one having a nervous breakdown. Anyway, I think I made the whole thing too absurd. I mean, having the Coppertone girl narrate? *G. damn!* What was I thinking? I've given them the psychological cover to disassociate what's happening on TV from what's happening in their own lives, but every plot is based on something one of them *did*. Also, I'm just going to say it: making Sonny black was a mistake. Maybe if we recast him as an older white guy, like a J.K. Simmons."

"Same old story," I said, edging away from Diana's reach, "everything we make sailing over everyone's head."

"Oh, that's funny. I didn't realize any of *your* work was going over anyone's head, or does *Affirmatively Consenting Babysitters 19* represent a real intellectual leap for the franchise?"

"Stop it, you two," said Maribel. "Different people, different approaches. That's all."

"I just think it's good semi-fiscal practice to point out that the one time we applied his 'pornographic cooking show principles' like he wanted, it cost Clara her job."

"Hey," I said, "that's not on me, that's on Paul Haggis. We inspired him to make *Crash*'s themes *obvious*, not *wrong*. I still cringe whenever I think about Sandra Bullock hugging her maid, as though that solved America's racial divide. But you know how it is when you're trying to stream your thoughts into an opinionated vessel. He had all these ideas and just wouldn't let them go. It all came out wrong."

"Could we please not talk about *Crash* for once in our G. damned eternities?" said Maribel, closing her eyes as she massaged her temples. "I need to be in the right headspace for this meeting. I've had a hell of a time getting in touch with G. lately."

"What's been going on?" asked Diana.

"I'm not totally sure. I keep filing permits to meet, but instead of responding through the usual channels he responds by sending me a screenshot of Taylor Swift's latest Instagram post with her follower count highlighted. I'm not sure if he's trying to trick me into going off-*Standards* by flustering me or what, but he should know I would never try to meet without a permit."

"So strange," said Diana.

"How many?" I asked.

"How many what?" asked Maribel.

"Followers."

"You're serious?"

"I mean, just wondering."

"64 million."

I whistled; Diana and Maribel glared.

We took our traditional cloud bench at the front of the Hall and turned to watch our colleagues streaming in over the bowl's edges. The pudgy trio from Animal Relations waved as they tumbled over the rim and onto their bench, far back as could be. Twenty rows up, the fratty crew from Natural Disasters gave us air fives and made the "kill me" motions they liked to make before long meetings (e.g., "hang me" by tossing invisible nooses around their necks, "shoot me" by cocking invisible guns and putting them in their mouths, "hara-kiri me" by ritualistically piercing their bellies with invisible samurai swords, etc.). While we exchanged pleasantries from afar, a pair of thick-rimmed glasses atop an angular nose slid into my field of vision like a bespectacled torpedo.

"Heeeeey," breathed Trent, eternally looking like he was searching for a more interesting conversation. "Been a long time, *muchachos.* Didn't hear much from the *choooosen* ones this semi-fiscal."

"Please kill me," I whispered to Diana, who grinned.

"Yeah, it's a *prooooocess*, Trent. Trentie Guy," she parroted. "Sometimes things land; sometimes they don't."

"You know… Same in our line of business as well, Diana. Very similar, indeed. But all thanks to G. above, a lot of big successes this year. A lot of *whaaaales* as the venture capitalists like to say."

"I'll bet," said Diana.

"Really connecting humanity, you know? They're engaging online in a way that's just never been done before. They're dating. Organizing politically. Sharing opinions. They sure have some opinions about your new show… *Filibuster!*, is it?"

"That's fabulous, Trent, just fabulous," said Maribel. "Is this your bench, by the way? Meeting should start soon."

Trying hard to look like he'd planned on leaving earlier, Trent donned the hood of his hoodie and flew back to the mass of bodies thirty rows up.

"Jesus," said Maribel, "guy inspires his first technological development since the light bulb."

When our colleagues found their seats, and their back-to-camp
yelps had resolved into a murmur, the Hall's retractable glass roof
ground shut. A projector beamed a light onto the now-exposed ceiling. When we looked up, we could see the Milky Way fade, replaced
by this bi-annual planning session's short film: the bottom of a pizza.
The pizza stood untouched for a few minutes, causing the crowd's
interest to wane as their murmur waxed into a din.

From the projection, an excited voice roared "Fee-fi-fo-fum!" and
a slice of the pizza left the frame, leaving behind some olives, pep-
peroni, and elongated strings of cheese. Just as we were beginning to
absorb the scene, a gigantic forefinger and thumb slammed into the
ceiling, blocking our view as they gathered the more essential toppings
(i.e., not the olives). Following some satisfied munching sounds, the
forefinger and thumb returned for a second slice, but as soon as they'd
picked it up, we heard a gasp, and the slice came crashing down. The
Hall shook. A pair of quivering hands entered the frame and cleared
away the remaining slices. From where once a pizza sat, a gigantic,
veiny eyeball now peered. The eyeball looked more terrified than terrifying, as it tried and failed to construct a new model of reality that
could explain what it was seeing.

The owner of the eye picked up the ceiling/plate and held us as
far from his body as his giant arms could stretch, giving us not only a
clear view of his gigantic nostril hairs, but also his living room, which
included a gigantic play place for his Giant son, who was eyeing his
father anxiously, muttering, "Fee-fi? Fee-fi?" The Giant looked away
and called out for somebody — "Fi-fo! Fi-fo!" — and we soon saw his
Giant wife run in wearing the universal wifely expression for "what
is it now?"

The Giant held up the ceiling and pointed at us, grunting a few

Gigantic phrases I couldn't make out, but his wife crossed her arms and hit him with a contemptuous look. The Giant looked pained. He slid to the floor and began babbling to himself: "Fo-fee. Fo-fee. Fo-fee." His wife threw up her hands.

"Screw this," she said, and walked back up the stairs, muttering to herself. "Thinks he's in *Gulliver's Travels*! Thinks a Lilliputian army is living in his pizza! My mother was right, the man is crazy…"

The scene flickered out as the projector shut off. The Milky Way returned.

"Hmmm. This one seemed darker than usual," I said. "Maribel, why did you inspire—"

"Shhh," she said.

A sinister energy pulsed through the crowd as a band of unemployed third-wave ska trombonists heralded the proceedings. The Hall rumbled. Light flashed. There was the slick, overproduced sound of thunder. The wispier bits of cloud from the cloud stage congealed, whirling into a vortex that went from gray to purple to white before falling away, revealing G. doing his best impression of the Creator from *The Creation of Adam* (which, contrary to popular belief, we had no hand in: Michelangelo was a dick).

"He must be feeling ironic today," said Diana.

"HEEELLLLOOOO, EVERYBODY!" said G., smiling with all the confidence of a man who'd completed an Executive MBA and a used set of Tony Robbins cassette tapes. "Thank you so, so much for coming. It has been a TREMENDOUS semi-fiscal here at *TGI*. MAMMOTH. MASSIVE. MONUMENTAL. GARGANTUAN, even."

The trombonists, savoring their first opportunity in years to contribute to something this misguided, punctuated each word with a trombone-y flourish. I mouthed the words "what is wrong with him" to Diana, who shrugged and began humming — louder when G.'s act became too painful; quiet and rhythmic when it seemed he may return to the quiet nobility of his familiar public servant's persona.

"Simply HUGE!" G. reiterated and, leaning hard on air quotes, continued: "Rather than do a boring ol' planning session this year, I thought we should 'Step Back' and reflect on our 'Accomplishments.' We'll follow up about plans for the upcoming semi-fiscal in our 'One-on-Ones' later, but for now, this meeting is about 'You,' because in short, most of 'You' are 'Crushing It.'"

Pretending to scan the Hall, he faked a flash of recognition and said: "Let's start with Natural Disasters! Natural Disasters — stand up! These gentlemen had themselves a year: private donations to developing markets at an all-time high. All-time! Let's hear it for Natural Disasters!"

The heavenly chorus, which didn't seem thrown by G.'s pea-cocking, applauded — nominally for Natural Disasters, but really, it seemed, to soundtrack G.'s grandstanding. Just before the applause completely died down, G. jumped into a shoulder-wide stance, put up both hands, and motioned the quieting crowd to hush.

"I think we've entered a parallel universe," Diana said before resuming her increasingly pained humming. Before I could respond, Maribel gave us a threatening look, so I agreed by humming all the more gratingly back at Diana. Maribel shook her head and began grinding her teeth, the mark of any seasoned mid-level manager in a large bureaucracy.

"Of course," said G., when you talk about big semi-fiscals it's impossible to forget Animal Relations. Is Greg here? Can Greg stand up? Oh, come on now, Greg — Greggie-boy — you know you deserve the shout-out... *OR HAVE WE ALL FORGOTTEN ABOUT THE EVEN BIGGER SHOUT-OUT THAT CECIL THE LION GOT?* How many anti-poaching signatures did we get, Greg?"

Greg, steadying himself against the Hall's rim, coughed. "1.2," he said.

"1.2 what?" asked G., frowning.

"1.2 milli —"

"*1.2 million!*" said G. "Huge, huge, huge. Thank you, Greg.

Let's hear it for Greg and team!"

As though to eliminate even the insinuation that it could be sympathetic to poachers, the Hall rumbled again, this time without G.'s help.

"And, best of all, it's a repeatable formula! Regal creature. Refined name. Feigned celebrity grief. I can't wait to see where Greg and team take the formula next!"

Seizing the beginnings of a frenzy, G. piled on: "And these aren't the only things that were huge! Political Corrections came correct with multiple regime changes outside of Egypt. Scientific Progress once again quelled any talk that the Earth is flat. Economic Development somehow launched *another* wave of food delivery services. Huge. Huge. And huge."

G. was now shouting over the applause: "Of course, none of these accomplishments would have been possible without the peerless agents of change from the Department of Technological Innovations. More people online than ever before. More connections being formed. More engagement. More content consumption. Media has become 100% social. We've got grandmas sharing memes on Facebook, professionals brand-building artlessly on LinkedIn, and depressed media personalities swapping journalism for tweets. We've got more novelty Instagram accounts than you could ever follow and more amateur YouTube content than you could ever watch! DTI's tireless work and steadfast dedication has empowered us to have our biggest impact on humanity since our inception. *Since our inception.*"

At this, Trent hovered in the air, high-fived his surrounding colleagues, and waved at the crowd. He pointed at G. again and again, as if to say, "It's only possible because of you!"

"It's only possible because of you!" said Trent.

G. let the applause die down naturally this time, which took a few minutes.

"Oh, and one more thing," said G., snapping back into his serious self.

Diana stopped humming. Maribel unclenched her jaw. *Finally*, I thought, *we can get back to work.*

"Sixty. Four. Million. Followers."

The crowd went wild.

DEMOTED

The meeting left Maribel, Diana and me feeling terrible. It wasn't that G. left out our accomplishments (we knew it had been a tough few years for our department), but that it felt eerie, like everyone was in on something we weren't. This was the topic of conversation as we flew from Cloud Hall back to Goodville to meet G.

"I dunno, you guys," I said. "Something about that just didn't feel right."

"Yeah — all of it," said Diana. "I don't even know what we're supposed to be doing. There is always — *always* — a whole planning session on the upcoming semi-fiscal's inspirations. This time he didn't even say if *Filibuster!* should get a second season."

"I'm sure G. will clear things up in a moment," said Maribel.

"Meanwhile," Diana went on, "Trent's team gets wiped up and down like they invented the television. Oh, wait — they whiffed on television just like they whiffed on everything else for the last fifty years before finally — *finally* — coming up with a 'Scalable Strategy for Technological Innovation,' i.e., stealing ideas humans thought of themselves."

"To be fair," said Maribel, "our work does occasionally seem to benefit from being shared on Agent Zuckerberg's platform."

"And what was with G.'s ridiculous *Creation of Adam* get-up?" asked Diana. "I don't know if he was trying to be funny or what, but it feels *really* passive-aggressive to have *that* meeting rocking *that* look given everything we've been through with that Florentine prick."

"Michelangelo has been dead for nearly half a millennium."

"And we're still hearing about him, aren't we, Maribel!"

"Look, I'm just as anxious about what happened. I didn't tell you this, but I didn't even get to consult on this semi-fiscal's short film —"

Diana threw up her hands.

"— and I've been doing that for the last seven thousand years. But we *must* believe that G. will clear things up in a moment."

"I dunno, you guys," I said.

We arrived at G.'s floor of Goodville, where we could hear the faint echo of a fly being zipped. "HELLO!" said G. as he wiped his hands on his *Creation of Adam*-style robe. "It is so wonderful to be with you."

He grinned and raised an eyebrow, waiting for us to respond to whatever it was he found funny. When he realized we wouldn't be responding, he finished his own joke: "AND ALSO WITH YOU!"

We let him hug us one-by-one, and followed him on the miles-long journey to his desk. Nobody spoke. When we arrived, G. snapped his fingers to summon three chairs. We sat down and waited for him to begin. He stopped and started several times before committing to a plan of attack, all the while stroking his Clausian beard:

"Look, you three, I have way too much respect for Inspirations to not level with you right off the bat. Your work, as you know, is near and dear to my heart. In many ways, I've always considered myself Chief Inspirer."

Diana coughed.

"But I think what we're learning — increasingly learning — is that it's a new world out there. Today's humans aren't interested in dissecting an involved investigative report or novel. They need — they crave — constant stimulation."

At this, a TV materialized behind G., on which superheroes who looked like Batman and Wolverine but weren't for copyright reasons began sparring.

"The point is: They're consuming too much content as it is."

"Content?" I asked.

"Content!" Wolverine growled as he took a swing at Batman.

"As soon as they're done with one thing they pop in another, and then another. Their heads are full at all times, with no room left over to reflect on the messages we're *interleaving* into the content. Trent gave me a very convincing presentation about all of this before we planned the upcoming semi-fiscal together."

"Wait… you already planned the upcoming semi-fiscal?" asked Maribel. "Because I prepared an entire Inspirations plan I was hoping we could finally discuss. One that I think will really shake people from their complacency. I've been workshopping a slew of new ideas for late night television that I *really* think will impact the upcoming election, but I was hoping to get your take first. I've filed a number of permits to meet, G."

G. continued: "Could you imagine a *Jeffersons* or a 95 Theses landing in today's media environment? There's just no way. You'd need to sum it up in maybe a few theses and you'd also need to pray they went viral. In a media environment such as this, we have to compete in a new way. We have to pump out continuous streams of content."

"Well, G.," Maribel said, "we can always adapt our strategy to what you've come to believe is a new world… or, uh, media environment. But we've never discussed this before, and you seemed to buy into last's semi-fiscal's strategy."

"And what was that again?"

Maribel paused, taking a breath so intense that it drew Batman and Wolverine's attention away from their sparring. They were now watching intensely.

Maribel continued: "Making movies about the financial crisis, continuing our 'Ethical Pornography' initiative, and, of course, producing *Filibuster!*"

"*Filibuster!* is a perfect example of what we're talking about here," said G. "It hasn't *done* anything. The US Congress continues to be as dysfunctional as ever, and Mitch McConnell remains an absolute ghoul. Clearly, they've found a way to separate what they're seeing on TV from their own behavior. And it hasn't caused people to hold their government to a higher standard, either. They just laugh and maybe — *maybe* — post about it on Facebook, saying something like 'lol we're doomed' before moving on to the next thing. You'd probably need to make spin-offs like *Gerrymandering!* and *Voting Rights!* before you could even make a dent in their real-world behavior, but how would you get funding for those? It's not like these are superhero movies."

Batman and Wolverine, who'd grown quite bored as G. went on, resumed sparring, producing *thwacks*, *grunts*, and *pows*.

"I suppose what I'm trying to say," G. continued, "is that in the past we've only been able to *nudge* the Zeitgeist. Now, thanks to Trent, we can *control* the Zeitgeist, and the best part is humanity doesn't even realize it's happening. It's total control but without the downsides. Honestly, the content is secondary. It could be anything. What's important now is that we *drive the conversation continuously.*"

"That doesn't make any sense —" Diana began, but she was interrupted by the loud crash of Batman throwing Wolverine onto a pile of empty barrels.

"That's why," G. continued, "we're — I mean, I'm — choosing to undertake the first major reorganization of *THOROUGHGOOD1* since World War II. Inspirations will now roll up to Technological Innovations so that we can capitalize on the bleeding edge synergisms between technology platforms and content creation. So that your work can have the greatest possible impact!"

We stared at each other, then at G.

"Look, you three, I know you're upset. Inspirations had a wonderful, memorable run as a top-level department. You went from oral tradition to books to movies to TV, even venturing into photography during that brief moment when people cared about it. You went from drum circles to records to MP3s. You nailed the transition from high art to pop culture. I mean, going from inspiring prophets to inspiring philosophers to inspiring Madonna to inspiring Madonna again? I haven't forgotten about any of that. But you have to admit that your approach hasn't resonated with today's technology-obsessed content consumer, let alone creator. I mean, Diana, even if you had a modern Dostoevsky to inspire, do you really think you could get him to write *Demons*? He'd be watching alt-right YouTube videos all day."

"*Filibuster!* is just as good as *Demons*," said Diana.

G. laughed. "The point is: media consumption habits change, and *THOROUGHGOOD1* needs to remain nimble. We need to foster a, uh —" A look of shame flashed across G.'s face, but he regrouped — "um, a startup's mentality. I learned all about this in my Executive MBA class last semi-fiscal."

"You went to business school?" I asked.

G. looked at me but didn't respond. At the time, I couldn't tell what his expression meant, but looking back on it now, I think it was sympathy.

Diana stood up to say something, but Maribel, ever mindful of bureaucratic norms, held up her hand. "Come on," she said. "Let's get out of here."

As we left G.'s floor, he shouted after us: "This will be your biggest challenge yet! It will be like that time Britney shaved her head!"

Back on our floor, the mood wasn't great.

"What the *fuck*," said Diana, stomping out a cigarette while pulling out another.

Maribel slumped in her chair, rubbing the bridge of her nose and staring at the tiny mountain of cigarette butts accumulating underneath Diana's desk. Normally, Maribel would ask Diana to smoke outside, but it was clear she didn't have the energy. Even if she did, Diana wasn't paying attention to us, but was flicking ash onto a memo she'd written a few semi-fiscals prior called "What does it mean to inspire the absurd in a world that already is? Introducing *Filibuster!*" In the memo, Diana argued that although she'd tried many times to use absurdity as a way of influencing humanity, her efforts had often failed because they weren't absurd enough. "To humanity," she wrote, "which is so incapable of intuiting second- and third-order consequences, a policy like 'Eye for an Eye' scans as profound, not futile. This mistake won't happen again: *Filibuster!* will attack the very concept of profundity, thereby making it an important counterweight to Maribel's political work, which even she would acknowledge tends to be more straightforward and overtly moralistic (e.g., *Daily Show, West Wing,* award show acceptance speeches)."

Although Maribel and Diana were eternally arguing about the validity of this approach, Diana wrote great memos and filed perfect permits, so Maribel would usually acquiesce.

I tried to cheer them up, but my clichéd encouragement (e.g., "when eternity gives you lemons, make lemonade endlessly," "eternity isn't about waiting for the storm to pass, but learning to dance forever," etc.) elicited nothing more than depressed half-acknowledgements. I couldn't blame them — the news was jarring, and not just because we were preparing for an eternity of inspiring memes and messy Facebook drama. You see, Inspirations and Technological Innovations had a history, one that went far beyond the occasional unpleasantry at semi-fiscal meetings. Indeed, the first conflict between our teams is what led G. to reorganize *THOROUGHGOOD1* the first time, long ago.

GENGHIS: NOT ONE OF OUR PROUDER MOMENTS

For centuries, *THOROUGHGOOD1* policy was focused on halting the rise of Genghis Khan. G. had never foreseen such a unique and potent combination of brilliance, bloodthirstiness, and virility, and he feared that if Genghis could unite the hordes, leave the steppes, conquer the world, and spread his genes throughout humanity, it would reverse millennia of glacial but hard-won progress. Your gene pool — already subject to manic, marsupial takeovers — would be permanently set back.

(At least, this was G.'s official reasoning. I think the real reason was Genghis's proximity to China and the Middle East, which were humanity's best hopes for art/culture/science/good governance. Which you could tell by contrasting their accomplishments — algebra, etc. — with Europe's, uh, "contributions," e.g., protecting female purity by developing ever-more-elaborate chastity belts. However, following our bungling of the Roman Empire, G. couldn't come out and *say* this since he was trying to placate a vocal minority within *TG1* that claimed he'd "FORGOTTEN ABOUT EUROPE," a sentiment they emblazoned on custom chastity belts that they wore while handing out pamphlets about G.'s relative listlessness when it came to combating Attila the Hun.)

It was into this anti-Khanic policy environment that G. spun up the Sub-Department of Technological Innovations — Trent's original team — in the early 600s.

The Technological Innovations team didn't have much of a

mandate, and at the time, G.'s management style was still quite lax. Thus, like any group of unsupervised boys, TI spent their first half-millennium figuring out fireworks. To be fair, this powdery preoccupation seemed sensible. TI was a support function, and the thinking went that it should do work that amplified ours. And so while Inspirations had always had a mission to modulate human behavior through creative inspiration, we'd now be able to add a technological flourish to our work.

The early returns to the partnership were promising. In focus group sessions, we found that the lessons of our court storyteller really landed when she dropped a firecracker during moments of danger, e.g. the protagonist fleeing from a dragon. Similarly, warnings of future famine felt palpable when accompanied by a blood-red firework. Even our more satiric comedians got in on the action, as Emperors didn't mind being made fun of so long as the risk of injury to the performer was sufficiently high.

These experiments made us confident that when push came to shove — or, more literally, when Mongol came to Wall — we'd be able to inspire leaders who'd heretofore dismissed concern over the Mongols as "Steppecessive," a portmanteau as lazy as their nonexistent preparations.

Things didn't go as planned.

"The steppes have been asleep for a thousand years," our inspired astronomer said, "but soon they will… *Awaken!*" A green and orange crackling firework went off behind him. "Meanwhile," he continued, "we remain asleep… oblivious to the looming threat!" A quieter, maroon crackler now went off.

"G. dammit," Diana said to Trent and me as we observed the proceedings on a projector screen from HQ. "I can barely concentrate on streaming my ideas into this astronomer. We went way too heavy on the fireworks. This feels really excessive."

The Emperor leaned forward: "This feels really excessive, Qing. Could you get to the point?"

"Yes, Emperor. Of course, of course. My apologies. My point is this: I've seen in the stars and in the planets that if we fail to prepare for the Mongol threat, our empire will turn… TO ASH!"

Qing unveiled a wooden model of China's northern walls. Across the room, his pimply apprentice sighed, lit a pair of fireworks, and plugged his ears as they took off toward the model, incinerating it in a pink-and-orange burst.

"Wait a minute," the Emperor said. "Do that again."

"Do what again, Emperor?" asked Qing.

"What you did just now. With the fireworks."

"Uh, sure… Yan?"

Yan removed a pair of fireworks from his bag and spun around searching for something new to destroy, but this proved challenging since a royal court isn't the optimal place to do your discount shopping. Plus, anything that looked budget, e.g., some shoddy tapestries, seemed to have been made by the Emperor's daughter. Yan wandered around the room, picking up vases, jade figurines, and the Emperor's daughter's half-finished paintings. Each time he did, he glanced back at Qing, who shook his head while mouthing the words "pick up the pace, you idiot." When the finance minister finally shouted, "No work ethic with this generation!" Yan ducked under a table.

The Emperor, worried that his point would lose its resonance if he allowed his court to get going about the sloth of 12th century youth, summoned two guards. The guards yanked Yan from his hiding place, dragged him to the center of the room, and tied him to a stake. They removed the fireworks from under his armpits, walked over to the Emperor, and aimed the fireworks at Yan, who was crying and screaming and cursing Qing's name. (Qing, meanwhile, was giving Yan a friendly thumbs-up.)

The guards looked up at the Emperor, who gave them a half-hearted signal to proceed. They lit the fireworks, whose fuses hissed as if to make themselves conspicuous. Throughout the astronomer's show, I'd been tuned into the Emperor's consciousness to gauge his reaction, but I now slipped into Yan's. The fireworks took off. Yan looked up. The last thing he saw before being annihilated was the shoddiest ceiling tapestry you could possibly imagine. I still remember the hopelessness I felt at the moment Yan's world went dark. I emerged from his consciousness gasping, like I'd nearly drowned.

"HOLY SHIT," said Diana.

"There's a crappy papier-mâché dragon right there!" I said.

"I think the Emperor's daughter made that for an art competition."

"But that tech!" said Trent, jumping up and holding up his hand for a high-five. "Pretty badass, right guys?"

"Ha! Hahaha!" said the Emperor. "Don't you see?"

The court, annoyed by the blood, guts, and pimply limbs this lesson had imposed upon them, waited for the Emperor to finish.

"We can use our fireworks as *weapons*. You really think, Qing, that a bunch of horse-riding Neanderthals from the steppes could conquer a civilization armed with *missiles*?"

Qing, whose ceremonial court robe was soaked in blood, scurried to the center of the room and bowed, avoiding the remains of his former apprentice and all the painful hiring implications they entailed. Continuing to half-bow, he said, "With all due respect, Emperor, this wasn't precisely my point. I'm no general, but I'm not sure this demonstration would translate to a real combat environment. With as much respect and grace as a man can muster, Sire… Yan was tied to a stake. Genghis will be, like, moving around."

The Emperor leaned forward. "Do you need another demonstration, astronomer?"

"Ah… no! Apologies, my lord, apologies! We are, of course, nothing but thumbtacks in your cosmic supply closet, and in my excitement, I may have pierced a photo that belonged in a frame!"

"What?"

"What I mean to say is… Your will is, quite literally, the rule of law!"

While speaking, Qing had been shuffling backwards toward the exit, but before he made it he slipped on a stray eyeball and tumbled to the ground, landing in a puddle of congealed blood. In a panic, he tried to get up, but each time he did, he would fall into an erratic, bloody Charleston that landed him on his hands, ass, or face. The third time (face), he stayed down and began sobbing into the remains of his former employee.

The court, who'd been dropping in and out of the proceedings all day, were at last entertained. They laughed and laughed and laughed. They praised the Emperor for his wisdom and toasted to their inevitable victory.

So, anyway, they were conquered in like a second.

For the obvious reason, losing 11% of humanity dragged G. down to a dark and diluvian place (somehow, in your accounts of Genghis Khan — none of which were inspired by us, by the way — you always seem to talk about his religious tolerance and how he totally made the Silk Road a thing, as though these qualities make up for all of the death). At one point, G. was so discouraged that he even thought about bringing in management consultants.

That's when Trent sensed an opening.

He donned a suit, read the last two *Venetian Business Reviews*, and in a dramatic, animation-heavy PowerPoint "prezo," argued that humanity was yards ("perhaps even meters") away from ceding market leadership to a troop of forward-thinking baboons out of Zambia. "That humanity's Jaunt with Jenghis [sic] would transform humanity's violent tendencies into full-blown proclivities." That G.'s "global leadership" would prove "globally indispensable" in tackling this "global issue."

Trent held up a napkin and continued: "Consider the case before us. By my calculations, Genghis was millions of times more violent than the average human being. For argument's sake, let's assume that 'Genghisianism' —"

"Gen-*ghisianism?*" said Maribel.

"GENGHISIANISM," Trent yelled over her, "impacts 1% of humanity. While I made up this number, I think we can all agree it's a very conservative estimate given Genghis's libido."

"Oh, come on!" yelled Diana.

"*This*," Trent yelled louder, "would *still* be enough to destroy humanity four hundred and forty times over."

Clara, who at this time was still leading Inspirations and had a particularly close relationship to G., thrust out her arms: "Come on, G., that's not how math *or* genetics work. We should be having a completely different discussion right now. The time is ripe to inspire pacifist art."

Trent opened his briefcase, removed a copy of *VBR's* "19 Management Lessons from the Desk of Kublai Khan," and dropped it on purpose: "Whoops!" he shouted.

Confident he'd drawn G.'s focus away from Clara, Trent went on: "Thankfully, I've got a solution. But it will require more direct influence than we're accustomed to."

G., who'd been sulking on his throne for twenty years staring at a McKinsey brochure, trying to summon up the will to call those smug know-it-alls, thinking he should probably change out of his pajamas before he did, wondering how he'd once again failed to stop the very thing he was most intent on stopping, looked up and took interest: "What kind of influence?"

"*Technological* influence," said Trent.

"But the fireworks didn't do anything!"

"That's because we've been thinking about technology all wrong. We need to stop thinking of technology as *support* and start thinking of it as *driver*. To do anything less would be a disservice to the 11% of humanity who died while we fiddled around with fireworks."

G. looked back down.

"Don't worry, G., this will work. Now, my plan *would* involve my team driving its own agenda. And this *would* be smoother if we were an actual department instead of just a sub-department."

G., who really didn't want to call McKinsey, said, "Of course…"

Thus, Trent's sub-department became the "The Department of Technological Innovations," and immediately began to spread opium around the world. This wasn't hard. They simply travelled from farm to farm spreading the word about poppy seeds, and your misguided penchant for chemical dependency did the rest. (Naturally, opium really took off in China thanks to the Silk Road y'all are so crazy about.)

G., preoccupied now by any threat of physical violence, was pleased: "Crime is *plummeting!*" he'd brag, pointing to his own graphs in his own animation-heavy PowerPoint prezos. "People are too high to fight!"

"And," Trent loved to add, "the economy is *booming*. Dilapidated warehouses are finding new leases on life by becoming opium dens, rejuvenating ailing communities and bringing in restaurants, condos, and private schools."

However, while G. and Trent were bragging about numbers, we in Inspirations were miserable. Our work — supposed to help you grow, supposed to help you ascend *beyond* your piddly human concerns and onto a plane of spiritual and moral enlightenment — could no longer stimulate your opium-addled minds. When we finally caved and met you halfway, we ended up producing painfully sophomoric stoner comedy.

I will never forget the confused and disappointed look on our fellow agents' faces when we premiered *Hustle & Hoe*, a musical about a farmer-turned-drug dealer-turned-pimp who smokes opium, owns a brothel, and yells his catchphrase "Cowabunga!" at random moments throughout the show. The whole thing was a creative low, but if I were to pick a true nadir, it would be the final scene:

Dante, our hero, reaches deep into the ass of Roxy, his girlfriend and former employee at Dante's Dimes. Roxy snaps and asks, "Did you find it, Dante?" to which Dante replies, "Yup! Turn around!" Thinking "it" is an opium-filled balloon (the plot somehow fails to address why they're smuggling opium in her behind), Roxy turns around, surprised to find Dante down on one knee holding a feces-crusted engagement ring.

"Will you marry me?" he asks, and Roxy, tears streaming down her face, says, "Cowabunga, Dante, cowabunga!"

Although I never asked her, I believe it was *Hustle & Hoe*'s closing line that finally spurred Clara to act. The day following the premiere, she stormed into HQ, gathered our department around her, and said, "It's time to fight back."

However, as anyone who's sat through a D.A.R.E. assembly knows, anti-drug campaigning isn't the world's most malleable creative clay. You can never tell if you should keep it factual or make it scary, and whichever you choose, it feels like losing. When Maribel inspired scholars to publish a pamphlet series called "Literally the Opiate of the Masses," we couldn't give the damned things away. And my contribution, a public health commercial about a couple who divorced because of the husband's opiatic ED, merely precipitated the first ever market for quack erectile dysfunction cures. Meanwhile, we got a ton of complaints from parents' groups when Diana inspired a famous animator to draw Jenny the Giraffe, a teenage giraffe whose neck got longer and longer as she got higher and higher until — finally — it snapped.

Worse, our campaign prompted DTI to wage an aggressive counter-campaign. Trent's techniques ranged from spreading misinformation ("we have *zero* evidence to suggest opium is worse for you than a cup of tea," a finding that came from a non-randomized longitudinal study comparing opium to opium-laced tea) to drawing his own cartoons (Henry the Happy Sloth, Zoe the Zany Zebra, Tony the Tilted Turtle, etc. — all amateurish, all massive hits with kids and parents' groups alike). When things got particularly contentious (around the time Jenny the Giraffe began turning tricks for opium money), Trent engaged in some *super* regrettable racial stuff encouraging Chinese consumers to relax by "slaying their inner Mongol," a campaign that preyed on so many issues of Chinese identity and masculine insecurity that it not only led to record opium usage, but also prompted the then-rulers of Ming-Dynasty China to rebuild the Great Wall, an undertaking that proved to be the world's deadliest pissing contest since the pharaohs of Egypt built ever-more elaborate tombs to show up their counterparts in Libya.

As the death toll for the Great Wall began climbing into Qatari World Cup territory, Clara became obsessed with planning our next move. We'd see her pacing around her office at all hours, until one day (around the time Jenny was kicked out of rehab), she called us in.

"We need to go negative. Jenny is close to bottom and I don't think her story is landing anyway. Maribel, I'm disbanding the Shakespeare taskforce so you can work on this full time."

Maribel, who'd been suffering from anxiety due to the unpermitted nature of our recent inspirations, said, "Clara. Please. We can't."

"We *must*. I've thought through every possible course of action, and this is the only one that gives us any chance of stopping this insanity."

"But we're doing so well with Shakespeare. It seems silly to give that up."

"G. dammit, Maribel, put Zeke on the taskforce then. When you've got a vessel like Shakespeare, the inspirer barely matters."

Thus, I inspired Shakespeare, and Maribel got the primary exporters of opium, the English, torqued on gin, an accomplishment requiring such minimal insight that it's almost embarrassing to admit. Given how polite Englishmen pretend to be, she simply inspired some ads that said "REAL ENGLISHMEN BUY THEIR MATES A GIN"; their inability to refuse a kind gesture — even one as gross as gin — did the rest. Suddenly, no one was sober enough to captain a shipping vessel. And while this *did* stymie opium exports, it also drew the annoyed eye of the mercantilism-minded Department of Political

Corrections. They realized what was going on, fought something called the Opium Wars, and reported us to G.

G. summoned all of us — Trent and DTI, Clara and DI — to his floor, with a note: "SEE, THE DAY OF G. IS COMING—A CRUEL DAY, WITH WRATH AND FIERCE ANGER...I WILL PUT AN END TO THE ARROGANCE OF THE HAUGHTY... THEIR INFANTS WILL BE DASHED TO PIECES BEFORE THEIR EYES."

Naturally, we tried to ignore the summons, hoping we could wait out G.'s anger by laying low in Europe, maybe inspiring the lesser known Impressionists. But G.'s biblical messages continued to arrive, growing stranger and scarier: "G. ANSWERED, 'BRING ME A HEIFER THREE YEARS OLD, A SHE-GOAT THREE YEARS OLD, A RAM THREE YEARS OLD, A TURTLE DOVE AND A YOUNG PIGEON.'"

When we arrived at G.'s floor, his administrative assistant came out to greet us, looking like a child who'd watched *Jenny the Giraffe* for the first time. "G. is ready for you," she said. "I did just want to say... in case I don't see all of you again... I loved Henry the Happy Sloth, Trent. He was so happy."

"Thank you, doll," Trent said. "Wait till you see this new animation tech we're working on. It's going to transform entertainment."

"Who's going to inspire the animation?" said Clara.

"Like it even matters."

We embarked on the long flight to G.'s desk, Inspirations and Innovations mutually trying to avoid eye contact. We could see G. — still miles and miles away — glaring, and even then we could sense his anger, feel his fury, see him trying and failing to find the words he'd use to condemn us. When we arrived, G. channeled the charred remains of a million discarded fragments that couldn't adequately convey his Old Testament wrath, and sighed...

(This sigh lasted four years, and you know it as World War I.)

When he finally murmured something, Clara and Trent leapt up to defend themselves, but G. held up a hand and shushed them. He shook his head, and sighed again…

(Complete breakdown of interwar European order.)

Once he'd calmed down, G. tried again: "Look, Trent, I realize you wanted to establish your department's brand, and I know we had some early success with the whole opium thing."

"We did, didn't we?" said Trent.

"But we agreed to drop it, remember? It was killing humanity's sex drive."

"*What?*" said Clara as she jumped up and slammed G.'s desk.

G. raised his hand. "Nope. I don't want to hear it, Clara. You can sit right back down. *Right back down.* As disappointed as I am in Trent, I am *infinitely* more disappointed in your team."

Worried G. may sigh again, Diana interjected, "We're sorry, G., we thought we were doing the right thing."

"Thought you were doing the right thing," said G., rapping his desk to draw Clara's glare away from Trent. "Thought you were doing the right thing?" He stood up. "Wouldn't the right thing be *not* to defy orders? Wouldn't the right thing be *not* to undermine another department's agenda? Wouldn't you want to *avoid* screwing up Sino-Anglo relations? *Avoid* betraying my trust? Wouldn't the right thing be *not* to lose focus on the *countless* issues you've missed in your quixotic, anti-opium questing? Do you realize you let Zeke inspire Shakespeare? *SHAKESPEARE,* for my sake. I don't think we'll ever recover from *Pericles!*"

"We just —" Clara began.

"And it's even worse!" G. said, slamming his desk with renewed fury. "I mean, maybe you *WOULDN'T* want to miss the entire bubonic plague aside from producing the *LAZIEST* public health jingle I've ever heard."

"Look, G., I know —" said Clara.

"Shhh. No more. No more. I think I'm losing my mind."

G. stood up, turned around, and sighed once more…

(Roughly: Everything from Germany's annexation of Poland through Pearl Harbor.)

Trent, meanwhile, was reclining in his chair, winking and pointing at us.

G. returned from his thoughts and spoke again, almost whispering: "You know, I suppose it's my fault. The world has become too complex to allow every damned department to run wild. I need to take a more active role. From now on, we're going to need *management*. A tops-down process. We need all of *THOROUGHGOOD1* working together — as a unit. As a *team*."

Thus, with these words, the modern *THOROUGHGOOD1* was born: centralized, semi-fiscal planning, all departments working together to fulfill G.'s strategic vision. And while this was a big change, we didn't have time to second-guess it: World War II was raging, and we needed to inspire *Rosie the Riveter* so women would build Trent's tech and thereby propel the Allied War effort.

We'd let things get a bit out of hand during our meeting.

NUEVO

Now, Inspirations was a sub-department, although we'd yet to internalize the implications. How could we? The last time we'd set wing on DTI's floor of Goodville, we'd been their equals, their colleagues. We'd been one-half of a powerful cosmic congress that would debate and pass judgment on the major issues of the day.

"We should bring back 3D glasses!" I recall Trent arguing. "If we don't, the derby scenes aren't going to *pop!*"

"Or," I remember Clara firing back, "we should *believe* in Tobey's ability to anchor the film's 143 minutes *without* relying on cheap drive-in theatre gimmicks. This is a *film*, Trent, not a 1950s horror flick."

"Fine. But then I think the horses should talk. We can CGI it."

"This isn't a dumb kids movie, either!"

"You're right. It's worse."

"You're worse!"

And so it would go, producing a spirit of aggrieved compromise that permeated not only *Seabiscuit*, but Tobey Maguire's entire iMDb. Now, that spirit was dead. Buried beneath a Kilimanjaro-sized mound of discarded 3D glasses bearing the visage of a superhero spouting an advertisement in a comic book-style caption:

SPIDERMAN: *Kellogg also sells me as a cereal!*

IRON MAN: *Kraft also sells me as a macaroni!*

BATMAN: *The private prison system is a critical driver of America's economy. Do you like cheap furniture? Cheap jeans? Cheap lingerie? If so, you're one of many consumers who benefits from the Thirteenth Amendment and its allowance for involuntary servitude in cases of pun-*

ishment for a crime. So call your Congressman and fight back — Boom! Kabam! Pow! — against the misguided attacks on this indispensable sector. We can't all be rich vigilantes, but we can all enjoy slightly higher purchasing power.

We arrived at Technological Innovations to find that the floor we'd helped to build as a post-Genghis peace offering was also dead. The exhibits we'd inspired, renowned across the universe, had been removed, components shipped to G.-knows-where. Gone, for example, was *pants pants EVOLUTION*, an evolving discotheque showing how the manufacture of clothing had progressed from fig leaf gathering to Dickensian child labor camps to Luddite-spooking looms to burning Bangladeshi sweat shops. Gone, too, was *THE BEER BUS*, which we thought might do something similar for booze but ultimately became a much more popular bus that served beer. They'd even removed *THOROUGHGOOD1* favorite *Fly Wars*, a playground that shrank you down to the size of a fly so you could navigate the innards of an evil, old-timey supercomputer, the goal being to lodge yourself in the computer's motherboard and prevent it from releasing a fly-killing super toxin, and also to gain a greater appreciation of technology. (It's possible the competing goals muddled the message.)

DTI had been equally ruthless when it came to revamping the floor's decor. No more cool, hovering, purple laser pathways. No more gleaming chrome desks or pulsing tubes of soft blue light. No more flying cars ferrying agents from one room to another. No more mile-wide mural summarizing humanity's journey through science and technology (a mural so good, even unbiased observers said it made the Sistine Chapel look like it'd been painted by a retired boxer). In short, the floor that was once a proud, shining, singular monument to progress (albeit one that embellished the role of fireworks in the grand technological scheme) had morphed into something stale, something lifeless, something terrifying. Something you might charitably describe as a Bangalore call center, not overdramatically describe as the slave encampment you'd find at a diamond mine, and realistically describe as beige.

Like super, super beige.

From the endless expanse of beige carpet grew infinite beige benches, upon which countless agents, uniformed in beige, hunched over their depressingly beige desks. Every few feet, a ten-inch hunk of semi-opaque dark beige plastic stuck up from the floor like a shark fin, dividing each pair of agents ("for privacy," Trent would later tell me), forming an infinite beige submarine that not even the Beatles could make fun.

"Wait a minute," I said, pointing at a nearby team of agents, "they're... human."

"That's weird," said Diana. "Totally against *Standards*."

"I guess G. must have given Trent his blessing?" said Maribel.

I stared at the human agents, trying to intuit the reasons for their presence. "It just seems... off."

We walked down the aisle until we found an agent who didn't seem to be working. When we approached him, he spun around in a panic. "I'M ON MY BREAK —" he began, but seeing a trio of unfamiliar faces, looked relieved.

"Yeah, we can see that," said Diana, motioning toward the agent's computer screen, where a knock-off Scooby was mounting Velma in some sort of adult cartoon.

"Hey, don't judge me. This is research," he said.

"Oh, really?" Diana asked.

"Yeah, I work on project *TOONY TAPIR*. We do something similar but for Disney princesses. Hey, have you seen *Ariel v. Ursula* or *Belle* v. *Lumiere*, by any chance?"

We shook our heads.

"Oh," he said, sounding disappointed. "Well, then, I guess you're not familiar with *CURIOUS CAT*. It guides people to our filthiest content by recommending increasingly risqué videos."

"Wait a minute," I said, "so you make porn?"

"Oh, yeah," he said, beaming. "This whole floor runs on porn, at least for now. There's been some rumblings that we're going to expand into new content areas. But we don't get much info out here."

"I don't get it. How could this whole floor only be making porn?"

The agent laughed and slapped his knees. He spun around to show us something on his computer, but began laughing again. He slammed his desk a couple of times and wiped tears from his eyes, and when he could finally control himself said, "Look here, guy."

He pulled up an infinitely scrollable page detailing his team's innumerable projects: *HORNY HORNET*, for example, used miniature black-and-yellow drones to spy on regular people making love, which it streamed in exchange for cryptocurrency. *VIRTUAL VELOCIRAPTOR* built VR versions of the Mambo No. 5 you could pair with any C-list-or-lower celebrity ("No one rich enough to sue," the agent explained). In a surprising turn, a project named *KINKY KANGAROO* merely dubbed Australian accents onto non-Australian videos, while *BESTIAL BUFFALO* did exactly what you'd expect.

'Ethical Pornography' was doomed from the start, I thought.

As our new friend explained the endless array of projects working within the Oedipal Complex, another agent — this one dressed in a darker shade of beige — ran up. "Hey!" she said, "What do you think you're doing?"

"Hi there — we're looking for Trent," said Maribel.

"Not you... *him*," she said. "Andrew, how many times have I told you? You don't have to walk every last trio of lost travelers through our work."

Andrew looked at the ground. "I'm sorry."

"And what do you think you're doing?"

"Are you talking to us now?" asked Diana.

"Obviously," she said.

"Uh, looking for Trent?" I said.

"You think Trent is *here*? That's possibly the most ridiculous thing I've heard today. This is Nuevo *East* Palo Alto. For gig economy laborers. What you want is plain ol' Nuevo Palo Alto."

"Wait a minute," said Diana, "Palo Alto is a town on Earth."

"Yeah, so is East Palo Alto. Trent says that together they form a perfect society, so he borrowed the names for his and added the 'Nuevo.' But if you don't want to sound like jackasses you should just call them Nuevo and Nuevo East. Anyway, as fun as it is to explain every little thing to you, I actually don't have all day."

"Fine," said Diana, "how do we get to *Nuevo* then? Just keep walking through?"

"Just keep walking through? Ha! Just keep walking *through*? That would take months. You'd need to walk through every shade of POV, DP, BBC, MILF, GILF, Great-GILF, Mega-GILF, *Ultra*-GILF —"

"Fine then," said Diana, "could you just tell us what to do?"

"Yeah. Go back to the entrance, find the 'I'm Feeling Lucky' button, and press it. It'll send you right through."

"Thank you," said Maribel.

"No problem." The agent turned around to leave, then paused. "One more thing: I wouldn't dwell too deeply on what you saw here. Trent likes to keep his gig economy as far out of Nuevo as he can…"

We pressed the 'I'm Feeling Lucky' button and materialized in a new environment. Behind us, we could see Nuevo East, now a beige haze. A number of security checkpoints stood in front of us.

The first was manned by an Orangutan named Seville, whose eyes were glued to a copy of *Big Ol' Baboon Butts Weekly*. He spoke without looking up: "What business do you have in 'No Beige Zone A'?"

Diana failed to hold back a grimace. "Look," she said, "we're just here to meet with Trent."

Seville flipped through the magazine until he reached the centerfold: a picture of a Baboon bending over and eyeing the camera seductively. Diana looked Seville up and down and walked away, huffing.

Seville finally looked up. "She looks sweaty," he said. "You all do… Hey, you're not gig economy, are you? There's a pool back there and gig economy workers can't use the pool. Not covered by our insurance."

Seville flipped to the next page, where a Mandrill was twerking on a Gibbon.

Diana, who'd inspired much of Jane Goodall's research and was likely contending with some serious cognitive dissonance, turned around: "Are you saying you're here to a guard a *pool?*"

"I mean, basically."

"Look," said Maribel, stepping between them, "we've had a long day, and we may be a bit grumpy. Could you please let us through? We promise not to use the pool."

Seville relented, and we passed through two more checkpoints: Checkpoint B was manned by a Gorilla named Zo scrolling through *BOBW: Digital* on his iPad, and Checkpoint C by a Capuchin named Petey watching *BOBW* on his augmented reality glasses. They were guarding a foosball/ping-pong table hybrid and a Nintendo 64, respectively.

At long last, we came to the fourth and final security checkpoint, this one guarded by a little girl.

"To enter," she said, "you must answer these riddles three."

"G. Dammit." Diana said, "We are way behind. Could you please let us in, little girl?"

"I am as old as the earth —"

"Is that a retort, or is this the beginning of a riddle?"

"— but as young as Rihanna's 'Umbrella.'"

"So riddle, then."

"I can be shallower than a kiddie pool but deeper than the ocean. Smaller than a book but infinitely longer. What am I?"

We sighed, preparing for the prodigious task ahead. We began to debate which of Rihanna's albums featured "Umbrella," but this went nowhere, since Rihanna's output is decidedly singles-centric.

"The iPhone," said a voice behind us.

We turned to find Genevieve, head of *THOROUGHGOOD1*'s Department of Sports and one of our favorite agents. She winked at us while putting her Nintendo 64 controller into her backpack.

The girl responded, "Yes. That's the easy one! Now get read —"

"Podcasts and cable unbundling," said Genevieve.

"YOU MAY ENTER!" the girl yelled.

On the other side of the checkpoint, we exchanged pleasantries and hugs with Genevieve.

"She doesn't change up the riddles?" I asked.

"She's an AI," said Genevieve, "but she never does anything aside from ask people the same three riddles, so she never learns anything new. Seems like an oversight, but what do I know? So what's been going on with you guys?"

We filled her in on G.'s decision to move Inspirations under Technological Innovations and our journey to see Trent.

"Oh yeah," said Genevieve, smiling to mask a frown. "Same thing happened to us."

"Whoa… even *Sports* is under DTI now?" I asked. "I can't imagine."

"Yeah, I mean, don't get me wrong. It's been jarring. My team is sad, confused, uncertain. They don't know — *I* don't know — why G. did this or what it means. And there's been some growing pains. Trent is planning to make us do some things we *completely* disagree with. I mean, can you imagine Terrance's face when I told him we'd need to help the *Cubs* win a World Series?"

We nodded sympathetically.

"He's been building up that curse angle for a damned century, and we thought we had two, maybe three more centuries before needing to blow that wad. We don't like blowing our wads prematurely —"

We nodded, suppressing giggles.

"But Trent showed us the numbers comparing baseball viewership to football and basketball viewership, and we realized we had to do something dramatic. We're thinking it'll be a crazily improbable Game 7 win."

"I'm confused," said Maribel, "how are you going to get permits to intervene in something like that on such short notice?"

Genevieve looked around and moved in closer.

"We don't need permits," she whispered. "I was confused at first, since that's *clearly* intervening in something of vast consequence. I mean, before joining DTI, we were just drawing up the paperwork for the Cubs to a World Series win in 2217. But Trent... he's doing something new. He's not *interfering* with free will, he's *channeling* it on a scale I thought was impossible. People are literally willing these crazy events into existence. I mean, how else could we turn around a franchise like the Cubs so quickly? It's *way* too unrealistic, but people don't want realistic anymore. They demand entertainment, and Trent channels that demand across an infinite number of people to make these things happen outside of the usual *THOROUGHGOOD1* process."

The four of us looked at one another, pondering the implications of what Genevieve had shared.

"And you know," said Genevieve, stepping away and shouting, "I would be remiss — positively *remiss* — if I failed to explain how much *simpler* things are now. In the past, we would need to spend days tallying up prayers before a Super Bowl, World Cup qualifier, or any game of pitz with serious political consequences. And not only would we need to *tally* them, but we'd need to remove any that were gambling- or Buffalo Bills-related. Now, Trent's computers can compute the popular vote automatically, saving *days* and *days* of agent time."

"Uh, that's great," I said.

"Why, it *is* great, isn't it?" she said, flicking her eyes toward a Smart Camera hovering a few yards away. "Plus, it removes us from the messy business of human sacrifice, which was annoying when humans played pitz and only became more annoying — inescapable, even — when Roger Goodell took over the NFL. Now, it's all up to the computers."

"That doesn't seem ethical," said Maribel.

"You know, 'Ethical' is funny. In a Ned Starkian sense, I guess it's not — he who doles out the punishment should swing the sword, etc. — but then again, does this kind of old-school ideal hold up in a world where culpability is diffuse and Arya is killing Freys by the roomful?"

"G. damn, I need to watch *Game of Thrones*," I said.

"Well, here we are friends: Nuevo! Your new home!"

If you could imagine the opposite of beige manifest as a town, you'd have Nuevo.

Neon green bike lanes looped around, through, and above shiny white buildings, whose Spanish tile red roofs shaded well-kept, happy-looking trees who waived at passersby and dished out compliments like, "Now *you* be the fairest of them all." Big mechanical butterflies flew to and fro, their loud-speakers playing the first two lines of Woody Guthrie's "This Land Is Your Land" alongside real-time tracking coordinates of the town's few homeless denizens.

"Avoid 37.44, -122.16!"

"Avoid 37.47, -122.16!"

"THIS LAND IS YOUR LAND."

"Avoid 37.48, -122.16!"

"THIS LAND IS MY LAND."

"Animated discussion happening at 37.49, -122.16. Avoid, avoid, avoid!"

"THIS LAND IS YOUR LAND."

"G. dammit, that's super annoying," said Diana. "That happens all the time?"

"Ha, that's funny, Diana!" said Genevieve, looking panicked, "the butterflies just keep the agents who work here safe and pumped up. Trent assures me that the agents here love the first two lines of this song."

While 'safe' seemed plausible, 'pumped up' felt unrealistic: Despite their colorful environment, even more colorful clothing, and the ubiquitous nature of this song whose first two lines they apparently loved so much, Nuevo's agents seemed weary, distracted, like some unknowable thing, some impossible responsibility, was draining them of their energy.

"They're working," said Genevieve, pointing toward a couple outside a coffee shop. "They're having a conversation, yeah, but see those glasses they're wearing? Half their brains are occupied."

As we came closer to the couple, I saw they had a stroller, where their baby was engrossed in a smaller pair of her parents' glasses.

"Wait… They're allowed to have kids?" I asked.

"Hard to stop them," said Genevieve. "They *are* human."

"Do you know why G. allowed Trent to hire human agents in the first place?" asked Maribel.

"Something about scalability and cost control? Frankly, it's been weird to have them around, but Trent says we need to foster 'human mentality' if we want something called a 'product-market fit.'"

"What are those pills they keep popping?" I asked.

"Addanax. A combo of Adderall and Xanax."

"So why does their baby's bottle say 'Addanax' on it?"

"Do you have to ask?" said Genevieve. "Nuevo has a huge youth mental health problem, but they have an even bigger problem addressing the root causes of serious issues, like the fact that they're always working and never see their kids. Hence: Addanax Baby Formula."

We arrived at the coffee shop and peered in to see an ornery, bespectacled clientele waiting for coffee. When one of them grew impatient, he ran his fingers along the tips of his glasses, sending a shock through the body of the beige-clad barista, who collapsed, seizing and spasming. The barista must have been used to this, since he dragged himself up by the chain connecting him to his pour over station and said, "Thank you sir. Your coffee is almost ready, sir."

Hoping to forget what I'd just seen, I turned toward the couple and waved at their baby, but she seemed preoccupied by something unfolding on her glasses.

"Hey, little girl, what's your name?"

"Please don't interrupt her," said her father, "she's doing her first unpaid internship."

"Look, honey," said her mother, pointing toward a Slivgon panhandling on the corner.

"Dammit, the butterflies must've missed him. And look — is he panhandling? This is terrible." At this, he covered his daughter's eyes. "I mean, it's one thing for him to *be* here, but there's a no-panhandling ordinance in Nuevo. He needs to go." Keeping one hand over his distracted daughter's eyes, he tapped the rim of his glasses three times, and in a moment, a driverless, rainbow-colored car called a PALLO came by. It honked cheerfully at the Slivgon, who summoned a painful mouthless sigh and staggered in. As the PALLO drove away, it passed a home whose white picket fence bore a banner: "YOU ARE WELCOME HERE," it said, in English, Spanish, Arabic, and Slivgonic.

"Where's he going?" I asked.

"Nuevo *East*," said the mother, "really a much more sensible *place* for Slivgons."

"I dunno, he seemed sad."

"It's a shame," said the father, talking over me, "I mean, the structural inequalities Slivgons have had to deal with. Systematic oppression over eons, you know. Acid-spewing, mouthless creatures in a basic world predicated almost entirely on speaking. I've got some reading material handy if you'd like to learn more."

"Uh, no thanks."

"Wow..."

They turned away in disgust and went back to their conversation.

"I mean, I would *love* to have the Nuevo East children at our schools," said the father.

"Of course, of course," said the mother. "That would be ideal."

"Well, ideal would have been better enforcing the 'No Kids' clause in their contracts in the first place. But now that they're *here*."

"Right, that's what I mean. Now that they're *here.*"

"We couldn't just have them *removed*, of course. That would be terrible for morale. We need to figure out what to do with them."

"And, of course, it would be *great* — just *lovely*, really — to have them at our schools."

"Of course."

"But we just don't have the resources."

"Exactly."

As the Slivgon was being wheeled away, another PALLO drove up to a sickly tree and stopped. The doors opened, and a team of thirteen arborists rushed out, surrounded the tree, and began to sing Ella Fitzgerald's "My Melancholy Baby."

"COME TO ME —"

"I mean, where would we put them?"

"— MY MELANCHOLY BABY —"

"It's better, I think, if they just start working immediately."

"— ALL YOUR FEARS —"

"Even if we could take them, I don't know if they could handle our schools."

"— ARE FOOLISH FANCY, MAYBE —"

"And it would be horrible for them to be discouraged."

"— YOU KNOW DEAR —"

"So early in life."

"THAT I'M IN LOVE WITH YOU!"

"Hmmm… T. damn this tree is depressed," said the leader of the arborists, "serenading it isn't working. We'll need the big guns."

He pressed the lens of his glasses, and in a few minutes, a second PALLO arrived. This one dropped off a boombox and a team of masseuses, who played a new-age didgeridoo track while rubbing down the tree with storming-Normandy urgency.

"The cambium!" the head masseuse yelled. "Get to the cambium!"

"Ah," the father said, "so nice we can keep the trees happy."

Genevieve, sensing now that Diana would punch the father in the nose, led us away from the family and toward the tree, who — despite his recent rub-down — still looked sad.

"You okay?" I asked him.

"I guess," he said. "It's just so hard being positive all the time, always coming up with new and topical compliments so people don't get bored. But where are *my* compliments, you know? Nobody ever says, 'Hey, great *Seinfeld* reference, Bruce!' or 'Ace throwback to *Ace Ventura*, Bruce!'"

One of the arborists looked up from his clipboard, sighed, and made a note.

"So your name's Bruce?" I asked, hoping to change the subject.

"Yeah, but the other trees call me Brucie." Without being prompted, Brucie continued: "I didn't always have sentience, you know. They gave it to me on a lark — which in my world used to mean 'bird' but can now mean '*zany, carefree adventure!*' Oh G., it's all some kind of sick joke. They must have thought, '*Hey, you know what would be great? If trees could participate in our economy!*' But then they realized, '*Oh, hmmm… well, it seems like trees are kinda negative, and they have no marketable skills, and they're only happy when they're spooking lone travelers in a dark forest. Well,*' they must have figured, '*this plan is still redeemable. Let's remove them from their forests and pump them full of antidepressants and have them sing to passersby like some performing monkeys!*' Oh, no, again with the nonliteral language. I can't help myself anymore."

Brucie began weeping. "I can't dole out any more compliments," he said between sobs, "I can't harmonize with the butterflies anymore."

"This tree may be irredeemable," the head masseuse said to the chief arborist.

"He's just depressed," said Diana, "you can't give up on him like that."

"Actually, we can," the chief arborist said, "for one, we can't ⠂

pour resources into a depressed tree ad infinitum. For two, he's not holding up his end of the contract."

"Contract? It sounds like he's being forced to live this life against his will."

"When we gave them sentience, we also gave them a choice: Accept the contract or become sawdust."

"Don't do anything, we'll take him!" said Maribel. "I mean, so long as there aren't any regulatory hurdles."

The arborist thought for a moment: "Well, I guess it's simpler than pursuing a breach of contract. Sure, take him."

"Okay, so... how do we do this?" I said. "I guess we could go grab a wagon or something."

"No need," said Brucie, who in an agonizing effort removed his roots from the ground and walked on them like a spider.

"Wait, you could have left the whole time?"

"Hey, guy, I signed a contract. I may have hated my job, but I still believe in the market."

"G. dammit," said Diana. "Can we be done with this *Wizard of Oz* bullshit? Let's talk to Trent and get this over with."

The townspeople went quiet, and the butterflies began blasting the tune to "Wonderful World." Everybody in the town joined in song, trees and agents and butterflies all:

> *I see pangs of pain, beige bruises, too*
> *I see them swell... and become blue*
> *And I think to myself, "Thank T., that's not me"*

> *I see skies of fear and clouds of blight*
> *The scorching beige day, the endless beige night*
> *And I think to myself, "Thank T. that's not me"*

> *The wealthy and connected shore up their power*
> *So that no one else's children have a chance to flower*

I see friends shaking hands saying "too busy bye!"
They're really saying "I'd poke out your eye"

I hear babies crying, I watch them grow
They'll be more screwed than I'll ever know
And I think to myself, "Thank T. that's not me"
And I think to myself, "Thank T. that's not me"

Maribel turned to Brucie and asked, "Holy shit. Does that happen all the time?"

"Every hour," Brucie said, sighing and shaking his crown, "just be thankful you haven't heard what they've done to 'Thong Song' yet."

———————

We arrived at Trent's home office — "the t-Dome" — following an ambitious journey during which we heard remixes not only to "Thong Song," but also "Trap Queen" and "Lemonade," whose revamped child choir chorus — *Should've stayed in school for a leg up* — made Diana weep and rend her garments in a heart-wrenching callback to both the Old and New Testaments.

The t-Dome was a big glass dome ("for transparency," said the guard out front) with a huge, lowercase 't' on top ("for Trent," he added unhelpfully).

(Subtlety wasn't a core Nuevo value, which we knew since a list of Nuevo anti-values was hanging in front of the building.)

"The glass is frosted," I said.

The guard shrugged: "Still more transparent than a wood dome, I reckon."

"And why is the 't' lowercase if it stands for Trent?"

He shrugged again and pointed to another anti-value: "SATISFYING EXPLANATIONS."

The guard knocked ("NOT KNOCKING" being one of the more specific anti-values) and the door shot up with a hiss. We entered the dome's single room to find Trent humming the tune to "Thong Song" with his back to us while typing on a keyboard. He spun around, winked, and pointed at us. *"Sing it!"*

We glared, glared, and glared some more, clearly not going to sing it even if Sisqo and Foxy Brown had been there to implore us. When Trent realized this, he raised his fingers to his lips, blew them like they were guns he'd just fired, and holstered them.

"Fine, fine, I thought you would be into it. Especially you three," he said, motioning toward Maribel, Diana, and Genevieve. "I mean, it *is* the Official Ladies Anthem. Foxy Brown says so right at the beginning of the song, but whatevs."

Diana, clenching and unclenching her fists, was fuming.

"How could you do that to 'Lemonade'?" she asked. "That's the best thing I ever inspired and you *ruined* it. That song took Gucci and me nineteen mixtapes, six studio albums, and one compilation to get right. We poured our *souls* into it, and you *killed* it."

"*Whoooaa there — hold the teléfono, hermana!*" Trent said. "We just gave it a tweak. It's a great melody and it keeps the agents pumped up and distracted from, well, you know. You should be taking this as a compliment. Don't be so difficult."

"*'Should've stayed in school for a leg up'?* It sounds like a low-budget commercial for a for-profit college."

Trent looked up.

"Oh. My. G.," Diana said. "You're using it to soundtrack a commercial for a for-profit college, aren't you?"

"I mean... In *India.* They don't even know who Gucci Mane is. Or Sisqo. Or anyone you've inspired. You've taken a very suspicious, US-centric, late-90s-to-late-aughts, white-male-Millennial view of the world, you know that? *Hey, is that a Strokes song I hear? Is that a reference to* Breaking Bad? *Hey... hey... do you like* The Wire? G. dammit. I'm trying to take you guys *global* if you'd let me talk for a damned second."

Diana spat on the ground and flipped Trent off. She spun toward the exit, but the guard outside was barring the door.

"Let me go!" she yelled. "I don't have to stay here."

"Ah, see, that's where you're wrong wro-wro-wro-wroooong," said Trent, in an appropriation of "Thong Song" more malicious than every fraternity band cover combined. "We're partners now, Diana, let's have a seat and talk."

"We're not partners!" yelled Diana.

"Well, I guess you're right. You're my *underling*," said Trent, filling the final word with spite. "So let's talk," he smiled, "like a manager talks to his managee. But before we do, I should say: hello, Gen! Thank you for guiding them to my office."

"Uh, no problem," said Genevieve, looking anxiously between Diana and Trent. "Just trying to help the team."

"Of course, of course," said Trent, "'LACK OF TEAMWORK' is one of our absolute strongest anti-values, as you know."

Genevieve smiled and nodded, waiting to be dismissed.

"Well, I should let you go," said Trent. "I've much to discuss with Inspirations. But before you go, I should ask: How are we doing on Tiger Woods?"

Genevieve frowned. "It's been a slog. We've been trying to rehabilitate his image. Trying to get him back in the swing of things, you know? But his public approval is at an all-time low — he's like a Congressman crossed with a journalist crossed with arugula — and it's making it hard for us to build up the social media energy we need to bypass the permit process."

"Ha!" said Trent, frowning and looking around his office. "What a comedian you are, Gen! A natural-born comedian! The permit process, of course, is alive and well — *alive and well*. We're not bypassing, merely *expediting*."

"Right... expediting. So, anyway, it still feels like more people are willing him into a drug-fueled sex relapse than a tournament win. It's horrible. Now that I think of it, maybe we can work with Inspirations to help rehabilitate his image? Maribel and I worked on damage co trol for Michael Jordan when people found out he a had a gambling problem. She managed to recast his gambling as being of a piece with his competitiveness. It was masterful. Tiger's PR team is an albatross. They keep letting him do interviews and I can't for the eternity of me figure out why."

"Well, you'll need to figure something else out. I've got plans for our newest subsidiary," said Trent, winking at us.

"Subsidiary?" I asked.

"Oh, yeah, we're doing away with the notion of a 'department.' Bit old-fashioned, wouldn't you agree? From now on, all of my departments are profit-producing subsidiaries of DTI Enterprises. I'm calling you Inspiration, Inc."

I frowned at Diana and Maribel, waiting for one of them to say something, but Trent had already returned to the subject of Tiger.

"And, look, Gen, there's a contingent of Tiger fans out there who just want things to go back to normal. Find a way to channel *them*… and also the PGA executives who'd benefit financially. Plus, it could always be worse. I could be commanding — uh, delegating you to popularize Slamball."

The color sank from Genevieve's cheeks, the vitality from her eyes. "We lost two good agents to Slamball."

"So then you should get back to Tiger! Thanks, doll!"

Genevieve, dealing with some kind of Slamball-specific PTSD, jumped up and down like an astronaut and waved at an invisible colleague: "STAN. STAAAAAN. NOOOOO. THAT TRAMPOLINE IS BROKEN. STAN NOOOOOOOOO." She fell to the ground and cried, bouncing up and down like, well, like she'd fallen on a trampoline. When the energy from the make-believe trampoline dissipated, Genevieve picked herself up, waved at us, and left.

During Genevieve's episode, I'd looked away as polite people do when another person is going through something difficult. When I did, I inspected Trent's t-Dome for the first time, and realized he'd decorated it with posters of what were ostensibly our most successful

TV inspirations, though I noticed that all the ones he'd chosen had somehow failed to fulfill their mission: Clara's *Friends*, for example, tried to stave off the burgeoning problem of loneliness and social isolation by modeling adult friendships but instead became a replacement for those friendships. Maribel's *The Sopranos* sought to expose the fundamental piteousness and destructiveness of masculinity by interrogating the depressing inner lives of members of a New Jersey crime family, but ultimately made a bunch of teenage boys think, "Wouldn't it be cool to be part of a New Jersey crime family?" Diana's *All in the Family* brought to the small screen a character named Archie Bunker, whose virulently racist and imbecilic ravings were supposed to throw a humorous spotlight on the absurdity of his worldview but instead gave a bunch of Nixon voters the cultural permission to buy "Archie for President" bumper stickers. My show, *The Walking Dead*, had the simple goal of convincing people that although humans could be bad sometimes it was still important to work together, but had devolved into an opportunity for viewers to rail against the stupid choices of the show's characters while bragging to their roommates that *I'd be so much smarter in a zombie apocalypse it's not even funny, bro, just you wait, bro. Anyway, whatever, time to stream some old episodes of* Friends.

Trent slapped his palms against his desk. "Alright," he said, clearly gearing up for a monologue. "Let's talk. First, allow me to bare my soul for a moment: You were right about opium. It was a dumb, dumb, dumb idea. As cool as the Silk Road was — that Genghis knew some things, didn't he? — it couldn't spread opium fast enough to undermine those damned social norms humans build: *'Don't smoke opium while you're farming.' 'Don't smoke opium while grandma's home.' 'Don't smoke opium, bla, bla, bla.'* I'm not saying opium had *no* impact — it did. But it was 1500 and people were *always* farming and grandma was *always* home. Imagine if we could have spread opium through a modern distribution channel: It would've spread like a new Ariana Grande song. The impact would've been boundless — *boundless!*

"Second, I hope *you'll* admit some wrongdoing: Intervening like you did, Jenny the Giraffe and all that, was also dumb. The blood of the Opium Wars — well, it was only Chinese blood, I guess. But I think it's safe to say it's on *all* of our hands.

"Okay, good? Good. The past has become prologue — or maybe it's become water under the bridge, or spilt milk. Anyway, the point is: While we jumped the gun on opium, my team *nailed* the Internet, which, in a roundabout way, seems to have brought back opium, but I digress… I mean, you saw our operation. It's vast; it's powerful; and above all, it's *not-evil*. It's keeping humanity *willingly* docile, *willingly* peaceful, *willingly* entertained — and it's doing so at the expense of their normally dodgy behavior. Teen pregnancy — down. Crime — down. Violent protests — down. Forming nomadic tribes and pillaging the resources of rival nomadic tribes — down. This is the best shot we've ever had at making humanity *thoroughly good.*

"G. sees it, too, and that's why he sent you here: We need you to up our game. As successful as we've been, humans continue to watch documentaries; they continue to take online courses; they continue to *read*, even. Things that may — if we're not careful — lead to *KFC…* Knowledge Followed by Conviction.

"We cannot — we must not — allow KFC to take hold… at least about anything too important, or anything they would feel empowered to do something about. Not when we're so close. That's why we need *you*. You alone can make our dream a reality. You alone have the knowhow to plug our content gaps. You alone can propel us from commanding a mere 73% of humanity's waking hours to 95%. You alone can give humanity what it's always thirsting for: *Something Better And Easier To Do.*

"That said, I should explain some things to all of you. You've seen the ratings and streaming numbers and aggregate box office take of your inspirations go down, yes? Don't protest now — it's all here, all in the computer. I replaced the Research Department with a Data Scientist and he made me some graphs, see? This is your average

Nielsen rating over time — it peaked somewhere around the time Maribel was inspiring the second season of *The West Wing* and it's been dwindling since. Look here: *Filibuster!* doesn't make a blip. *'Oh, but how about all the 'Conversation' it sparks?'* Right? *'That has to be worth something.'* Well, here are humanity's DMs, IMs, blog posts, phone transcripts, and — my favorite — voice recordings logged by smart appliances. So what do we see? Radio silence. *4'33"*-level quiet. Less buzz than a beehive suffering from colony collapse.

"Even if you limit the query to Washington, D.C., there's only a single bar where people care. And they all appear to be low-level aides who gather so they can watch while playing drinking games. It *is* true, Diana; there's even a set of rules. Whenever someone says 'Filibuster!' or makes a melanin pun (their favorite so far is Melininania), you do a 'Presidential Body Shot,' which, I guess, is a regular body shot but you do an impersonation of an ex-President before you take it. I mean, look: It's all here according to this algorithm that picks up on irony and drinking game rules, as well as this video of a guy downing a shot after he says, *'I'll down this body shot like I downed Ricky Ray Rector to prove my Tough on Crime bonafides.*

"Agreed — completely in poor taste. But they're hammered. And this is the cream of your show's conversational crop! When we sent down our resident psychoanalyst for some qualitative follow-up, two things happened: (1) He produced a report arguing that you'd 'essentially recreated Archie Bunker, this time for D.C.'s professional-managerial class, failing to accept (yet again!) that satire is always and everywhere outrun by nihilism, which allows audiences to not only accept the satire's purportedly farcical precepts, but to embrace them. In *Filibuster!,* Agent Diana has given these aspiring Senators and lobbyists the permission to swap any lingering *noblesse oblige* they might've had for cut-rate Machiavellianism. 'Greed is good,' but for Beltway social climbers.' (2) He quit.

"And I don't even mean to pick on *Filibuster!,* or *Fill-a-Crap!* as the Young Republicans call it. This is all emblematic of a much larger problem I can help you fix: Y'all are way too highbrow for today's human. Y'all need to give the people what they want.

"For example, Maribel: do you realize how much time your department has spent inspiring *jazz* musicians lately? Look at this pie chart. Jazz musicians, for G.'s sake! Can't you see everybody was only *pretending* to like jazz? You thought people were responding to the power of the sublime, but what they were really doing was trying not to seem dumb. Now that they have limitless options, humans aren't going to hang around waiting for a *coda* or comment on a sweet motif — they're going to mainline sugary songs that are nothing but super long choruses, which is a trend you straight-up missed. No, it's not dramatic, Maribel: Look at this graph — popular songs are now 75% chorus. You're like a teacher assigning homework to a group of students on permanent recess: They're not going to listen!

"I have a theory: I think you've been trapped in the Shakespeare Paradigm since you had that run in the early 1600s. You've become the post-Michael Jordan NBA — always hunting for the Next MJ, the Next MJ, the Next MJ. Always hunting for *talent*. But I would argue that you took the wrong lesson from the early 1600s. The lesson wasn't that we need to find ourselves more Shakespeares, more Michaels. That's a fool's errand, because even if you land the occasional Vince Carter, you're mostly going to end up with Harold Miners, who, sure, can throw down a mean slam, but is he ever going to win you a championship? The lesson *should* have been: 'We (via Shakespeare) controlled the Globe Theatre. We (via Shakespeare) owned the sole distribution channel. We (via Shakespeare) were the only show in town.' I mean, what kind of theatre company even has the capital to build a theatre in Downtown London? You should've realized you were dealing with a black swan.

"Now, you're one of *many* swans — and therein lies the rub. Do you think your early-1600s slob would have preferred Shakespeare to, say, Toby Keith given the choice? Of course not. If Toby Keith had penned a "Courtesy of the Red, White & Blue"-style anthem about

Agincourt, no one would have cared about *Henry V*. Look at your biggest successes. They all involved a rare confluence of talent and distribution: Shakespeare and the Globe. Socrates and the Agora. Lil Wayne and DatPiff. And by now, you must sense these confluences are dead, gone — the game is up. All the world's become an infinite stage, all the YouTube stars and self-published authors and partisan journalists merely streaming.

"Do you not find it at all suspicious that we haven't engaged you on a project since *Seabiscuit?* That we haven't *collaborated* since you inspired indie rock musicians to soundtrack iPod and iPhone commercials? The truth is: We haven't needed you. Even works of art that would once have required significant Inspirational resources can be made in a lab now. For example, we have an AI that takes comic books as input and outputs superhero movies that maximize average engagement, where 'average' is weighted by total family income and so can basically be thought of as a fourteen-year old upper middle class American boy. Which, at bottom, is all anyone aspires to be anymore: rich and fourteen!

"But that's not to suggest you're useless now! No, no. Your greatest act is ahead of you. See, people are consuming garbage, but they don't want to *think* of themselves as consuming garbage. Fools, as you know, doth think they are wise. They're *about* to put on a jazz record, they just want to hear this new Taylor Swift chorus everyone's talking about first. They're *about* to grab a book from the teetering pile of books on their nightstand, just after they reread *Harry Potter* so they can follow that weekend's *Harry Potter* movie marathon. They're *about* to watch that documentary, they just need to relax with a few hours of bland, interchangeable Netflix programming to get themselves in the right headspace.

"They're About To. About To. About To. And while About To is a good start, it's not an equilibrium. I don't *think* the Abouteers will follow through, but they might — and that's where you come in. In the same way the NBA embraced small ball, corner threes, and the shoot-first point guard, you need to embrace your new role: In a world with infinitely many Globe Theatres, *Validation* — not talent — is the new Shakespeare.

"You're going to help us turn restless into relaxed, concerned into complacent, striving into sedentary, About To into Never Going To. You, *hermanos*, are going to change the world."

Brucie, who had continued to hang around for some reason, said, with a shockingly clear grasp of our mission, "But T., if Inspirations doesn't lead, then what's the point? Sure, sometimes when they lead you end up with simplistic, self-satisfied PSAs." Brucie coughed, mumbled "*Crash*," coughed again, and continued: "But sometimes… Sometimes you end up with something beautiful, something profound, something like *Apocalypse Now. Brokeback Mountain. Con Air. Clueless.* Surely, these are worth saving?"

Trent shook his head. "Can't you see, Brucie? We don't need to lead anyone anywhere anymore. In the eons-long struggle to prevent humanity from consuming itself, we've drawn a royal flush: all we need to do now is play our hand."

"But Trent," said Maribel.

"Call me 'T.'"

"But… T.… it seems like all you've been doing is making pornography more niche and sporting events more heartbreaking. Don't these things drive humanity apart?"

"G. dammit, guys, it's like you're not hearing. We need you to transform everyone's idiosyncratic media consumption bundles into their own personal fetishes, their own personal World Series victories. They need to believe that there is *nothing* more meaningful or more profound or more consequential than the individual 'choices' they make about what content to consume. They need to live in their own little perfect worlds that prevent them from seeing how messed up the real one has become. If they don't, they might try to change things, and who knows what chaos might emerge then?"

"But, surely, there remains something beautiful about shared experience."

"Surely, though, you are wrong. Shared experience has always been bunk. Just ask the Russians how much they 'shared' in Neil Armstrong's walk-a-bout. Look, the evidence here is insurmountable. The more validation we give to people, the more docile they become. I thought you were on board. If I have to go to G...."

"Alright, alright. G. dammit," said Maribel. "How do we go about 'digitally validating' people's choices?"

"Now we're talking; I'll give you your assignments, but let me warn you: They're tough. We've put our top agents on them and... Nothing." Trent turned empty palms upward. "Which is why G. sent you and why we need you. Maribel, you're going to inspire politically high-minded recaps of reality television shows. Diana, you're going to inspire sponsored content for critical advertisers. And you," he added, pointing at me, "you, my friend, will supervise."

"Me?" I asked.

"You," Trent said.

"What? Why?"

"I think you have the intangibles. Who did you think I was addressing during my whole spiel up there?"

"I thought the general 'you.'"

"No, you — I was talking to *you*."

"Uh, no, thank you. I think Maribel should be in charge. She's a great boss. Fair, transparent, supportive — "

"Screw Maribel, guy!"

"Hey, I'm right here," said Maribel.

"Look," he said, ignoring Maribel while staring wildly into my eyes. "This is your time. I've seen your work, and I've seen the rest of your team's work, and *yours* is what we need. *Yours* is what the market demands. You grok, in a way no one else can, that punchlines only land when they're step-on-a-rake obvious. That porn dialogue is the best dialogue. That themes can't be subtle or draped in unsympathetic absurdist trappings like *Filibuster!* You accept, in a way no one else does, that challenging people is pointless, that they want what they want, and even if that means we sometimes need to turn a song like 'Lemonade' into a soulless jingle selling seats at a for-profit college, we need to meet people where they *are*, not where we *wish they were*."

"Plus," he said stepping back, "your specialty was porn, and I think you know we've got that covered. So… you in, *hermano*?"

INSPIRATION, INC.

I needed to learn how to manage — quickly — but I ran into an immediate problem. You see, we never inspired any books on management, as we took Keynes at his word that this capitalist blip was a seedy rest stop on the expressway to a post-scarcity economy ("best," he said, "to shut your eyes and plug your nose while you deuced"). When I raised this to Trent (minus the bit about deucing), he handed me a pile of your management books, explaining how much he loved them and how they'd already prompted G. to begin "re-paradigming" *THOROUGHGOOD1*'s stodgy, paternalistic management style.

"Sooooon," said Trent, "they'll help you do the same, *jefe*."

I was terrified. Say what you will about our work, but whenever we leave things to you, they inevitably go worse: nu-metal; third-wave ska; conscious rap; pre-Bach Baroque. (We spent a lot of the 90's and early 1600's playing the stock/tulip markets.) But I couldn't see a way out, so I read. The competing, conflicting, erratically formatted messages still haunt me.

Some books said, "Hey, let your employees do what they want — **an empowered employee is an efficient employee!**" while some said, "It's about <u>Metrics</u> — you can't keep your employee efficient if you don't <u>ME</u>asure what he's doing!" Some books said, "YOU NEED TO BE A CAPITAL 'L' LEADER," while some — in a confusing, pedantic distinction — disagreed, stressing "one mustn't confuse **leaderSHIP** with **manageMENT**: leaders *in-SPIRE*, managers get *re-SULTS.*" Usually by way of a crude chemistry analogy, a distressing many recommended you form weakly held emotional bonds, e.g., "These prompts will show your team you take a capital 'I' *Interest* in them: 'How was your weekend?' 'How is your [hobby] going?' 'How was your [son/daughter]'s [activity]?' 'When is your vacation?' 'Can you make it shorter?'" Then again, other books demurred, pointing out that "The '95/96 Bulls weren't **Friends.** They were a **Team.** If you want friends, join a **Bowling League. Bowling Leagues** aren't efficient. The '95/96 **Bulls** were." Tangentially, a number of old books claimed, "for maximal efficiency, you must build your team like the Greeks built phalanxes," while more recent books said, "No No NO — that was all wrong — capital 'D' <u>DIVERSITY</u> is the key — so long as it comes with the same undergraduate schooling." Some books said *"CREATIVITY* is what you need to compete" while others said *"STRATEGY* is what you need to compete" while others said *"TEAMWORK* is what you need to compete" while others said *"CROSS-FUNCTIONAL* is what you need to compete," and for some reason, these pronouncements would usually come with an equation, e.g., Efficiency = Creativity^2, Efficiency = Strategy^2, Efficiency = Teamwork^2, Efficiency = Cross-Functional^3. A number of books stressed "Mission," claiming *purpose* could help you carve out a profitable niche (e.g., Tom's Shoes, Spanish Inquisition). Meanwhile, Buddha — great guy — would have been acutely aware of his dismay at seeing mindfulness reincarnated into a booklet called "10 WAYS MINDFULNESS WILL BOOST YOUR BOTTOM LINE." And, indeed, many of your most famed management theorists loved bastardizing beautiful ancient ideas. Among gurus who'd taken exactly one philosophy class, for example, Stoicism was the preferred ally in the pursuit of profit — especially if you had to fire somebody: "Marcus Aurelius asked, *'Don't you see the plants, the birds, the ants and spiders and bees going about their individual tasks, putting the world in order, as best they can? And you're not willing to do your job as a human being?'* I'm sorry, but we're going to need to let you go." A small, Epicurean backlash followed, but this being a smaller movement among gurus who'd taken *two* philosophy classes, the result was minimal: a few ping-pong tables and bean bag chairs at a couple of well-funded, monopolistic technology giants. Much more interesting was an extensive literature that boiled down the success of a company or individual to a single factor — M.J.: **GRIT.** The Wright Brothers: **GRIT.** GE: **GRIT.** The '95/96 Bulls: **GRIT.** Ford: **GRIT.** Enron: **GRIT.** The '96/97 Bulls: **GRIT.** Comcast: **THE TELECOMMUNICATIONS ACT OF 1996.** Initially, I was impressed, thinking this genre a savvy ironic commentary on how survivorship bias could hijack your love of simplistic narratives to produce erroneous and dangerously crude conclusions, to show that maybe — just maybe — the secret to management, as with so much else, was humility.

But then I found out you were serious.

Eventually, I could see that despite these superficial differences, despite the contradictory equations for efficiency, despite the uniquely tortured invocations of different famous athletes and coaches, your management texts were more similar than different:

They all began with Wayne Gretzky's famous nothingism, "Don't skate to where the puck *is*, skate to where it's *going*" (failing to acknowledge that the real corporate elite could push the "puck" toward tax loopholes, corporate welfare, and anti-competitive regulation). They all had names consisting of a single word, then a colon, then a long, pointless elaboration (e.g., *Competition: Why We Love to Compete, Pants: How They Came to Rule the Modern Workplace, Poor: Why It's Their Fault*). They all took a single, simple analogy you could explain in like four paragraphs and relayed it over exactly 287 pages (which is how you wound up with MLK's socialist awakening being compared to New Coke, and — in a horrible extension — his assassination being compared to Coke's return to Coke Classic). Finally, if the authors of these books were being honest (which, of course, they can't, given that they say things like "win-win" and "dominant paradigm" unironically), they would acknowledge their direct intellectual lineage to the first book in Trent's pile, Frederick Winslow Taylor's opus *Principles of Scientific [sic] Management*.

This 1911 book famously asked: *How many tons of pig iron could a "large, powerful Hungarian" move if a "college man" timed the Hungarian with a stopwatch?* The answer? Well, assuming Hungarians were automatons ("if only," Taylor might have said), each would move 75 tons per day, but, of course, one had to account for lunches and bathroom breaks and human frailty, so Taylor lowered the rate by 37% (to 47 tons per day) in humanity's first ever bragged-about case of Fudging, which many think is a *limitation* of management consulting when in reality it's the whole damned point, since it ensures that only The Right Sort — those who can say, without shame, "This 37% adjustment is based on our wisdom and experience," "This merger will produce 5% more revenue due to cross-selling opportunities," "There is a 100% chance that there are WMDs in Iraq" — can administer these coded ministerial protestations, and indeed, your so-called Skills Gap, which claims that "people can't get jobs because they don't have the skills," is in reality a symptom of how, in an economy where everyone is everywhere Fudging, you've run out of Elite Fudge Scoopers, run out of The Right Sort, so you resort to graduates of state schools or first-generation college graduates or minority women who don't know how to play the game, who are *doubted* when they say "37%...", "5%...", "WMDs...", etc., but, of course, The Right Sort fancies itself inclusive and so it must cope-cope-cope, concocting a story about skills-skills-skills in yet another example of Fudging run amok.

Thus, the lasting achievement — the genuine triumph — of your management texts is that they found ways to put cosmopolitan lipstick on their pig iron roots. They knew that in its raw formulation — "How many tons of pig iron could a large, powerful Hungarian move if a good college man timed him with a stopwatch?" — was dehumanizing for Hungarian and college man alike, that only a sociopath could stomach this question without some "paradigm shifting"

— or at minimum some light "reframing." That to continue earning consulting fees and fostering the development of a professional-managerial class, they would need to obfuscate.

And so: While the premise remained — that pig iron/report/ sales lead wasn't going to move/write/generate itself — the instrument of control did. The stopwatch became the eight-hour work day. The stopwatch became the permission to decorate your cubicle. The stopwatch became empowerment. Became diversity. Became creativity. Became the looming specter of outsourcing. Became capital 'M' "Mission." The stopwatch became the appropriation of an ancient practice whose purpose was to develop self-knowledge and wisdom that would ultimately lead to the freedom from all suffering (and also seemed to increase the rate at which you produced reports).

Crucially, these developments *solidified* (rather than weakened) the Winslow Taylorian, uh, paradigm, whose hold over the culture was complete even before becoming broadly palatable. Indeed, World War I may have been the first Winslow Taylorian conflict, the point at which human life was finally reduced to simple statistics: As early as 1914, military leaders realized that *exhaustion* — not conquest — would determine who won, that the conflict would not be resolved through strategic or tactical brilliance, but by killing more of the enemy than you yourself lost. And so war became routine, expressible in equation, in ratio: Number of lives necessary to take five miles of land (44-70K Brits per mile at Passchendaele); number of lives lost per enemy combatant killed (1.13 Frenchmen per German at Verdun); number of weeks a soldier could be at the front before going insane (2-3 weeks); number of Armenians who had to die (most of them).

Which all, of course, begged the question: "For what? Why? What was it for?"

For pig iron.

So France could once again produce wine in the Alsace-Lorraine. So Japan could grab some Shandong. So New Zealanders could vacation in German Samoa. So France and Britain could Sykes-Picot some oil-producing territory in preparation for a future conflict. So the Allies could build a "League of Nations," a fancy new building where good college men could host cocktail parties and devise new innovations for pig iron movement. The reasons were cheap, but the problem could never be the reasons, the pig iron: Winslow Taylorian thinking wouldn't — couldn't — allow it. The problem had to be one of capital 'M' "Messaging": the casualty counts looked *unseemly* when you compared them to the cold, ruthless exchange of territory changing hands. The equations couldn't account for human feelings and sensitivities, for dignity.

Management theorists took notice and cleaned up the messaging for WWII by emphasizing the Western Front and Hitler instead of what it was like to be a Central or Eastern European when the Germans and Soviets were really going at it, *Band of Brothers* being a more stirring story than *Cannibalism in Leningrad* or *Rape in Berlin*.

Incidentally, the US military now practices mindfulness.

Ah, and I forgot to mention the one thing your management theorists actually agreed on: When a subordinate gets promoted over his former colleagues, things turn to shit.

Feeling uneasy about what management seemed to ask of managers, wondering if I could live the endless bunk, baloney, and hokum I'd consumed, I opened the final book Trent had given me, a book he'd made sure to separate from the others. It was called *BATNA: Best Alternative Means to a Negotiated Agreement*, and it explained how, in any deal-making process, you needed to know your fallback plan.

I realized I didn't have one

Thus, I combined the least noxious elements of your management books into a schizophrenic management style that I can't say I'm proud of. I *empowered* Diana and Maribel to choose their own assignments, but when they chose incorrectly, I *re-empowered* them by making them choose again. I gave them maximum flexibility in terms of where and when and how they did their assignments, but bought a pair of walking, talking stopwatches to keep them on track. I explained that Efficiency = Accountability^2, and that Accountability = Metrics + Goals + Stopwatches (implying that Efficiency = Metrics^2 + Goals^2 + Stopwatches^2 + 2 x (Metrics x Goals) + 2 x (Metrics x Stopwatches) + 2 x (Goals x Stopwatches), but don't think about that too much), so we should shoot for one inspiration per hour.

When Diana and Maribel complained about this, saying I'd become a tyrant, I engaged in some *active listening,* thanked them for their feedback, and suggested we go to ice cream as a bribe/team-building exercise.

"I'll have vanilla and caramel topping," said Diana.

"Banana chocolate for me, thank you," said Maribel.

"Do you have UB40?" asked Cogslow, one of our stopwatches.

"Band, lubricant, or swirl?" the shopkeeper asked.

"Band — oh, but could you top that with gears?"

"Same for me!" said Bezelina, our other stopwatch.

The shopkeeper removed an old music box from under the counter, smashed it, and sprinkled the gears over the "Red Red Wine" third of the UB40 ice cream.

When everyone had been licking their ice creams for a few moments, I coughed and said, "So, uh… This is fun, isn't it?"

"You aren't going to get anything?" Diana asked.

"Just being with my — or is it *our* — team… is, uh, good enough for me?" I smiled and coughed again.

Diana shook her head and turned to Cogslow and Bezelina. "So," she said, "what did you do before you were our stopwatches?"

"Well," said Cogslow, "we come from a country named Crownswell, where we lived in a small village named Gearston."

G. dammit, I thought.

"Our life there was simple and traditional," said Bezelina, "real 'sand of the hourglass' type of existence."

"Timekeeping there wasn't *for* anything. It just *was.*"

"Oh, yes," said Bezelina, "it was sublime. We timed everything. Our children would time simple things: Dogs barking, dragonflies flying, dolphins diving, squirrels scurrying up trees. And we would time more complicated things."

"The time between seasons, say, or the average length of a sitcom episode sans commercials."

"And our king — a good and kind and *wonderful* grandfather clock named King Crownswell — timed *epochs*: Bronze, Iron, Middle. Permian, Triassic, Jurassic. New wave, Synth pop, Chillwave."

"But then," said Cogslow, "something changed. King Crownswell sensed it first, but slowly, we all began to feel it. A new epoch had begun."

"One in which timekeeping wasn't a sidecar companion on the scooter ride of progress..."

"But a *determinant* of progress."

"Time was the perceived blocker of life, something to be optimized away."

"And timekeeping," said Cogslow, "was the perceived solution."

"No longer, then, was it sufficient to merely *time* a cheetah downing an impala. To *time* Sheryl updating that report. To *time* how long a subgenre of rap or metal or indie music lasted."

"Timing had to lead to *results*. The cheetah needed to run superior routes. Sheryl needed to stay in late. And the latest fusion of grindcore, sludge, and technical death metal needed to give way to something new."

"Maybe blackened witchrap deathstare glammetal fuckdeath," said Bezelina.

"Indeed," said Cogslow. "Lest the impala get complacent. Lest Sheryl see her kids. Lest music critics get bored. Timekeeping had to move from passive to active, from independent to accelerant. Life became a race to witchrap deathstare glammetal fuckdeath."

"And obviously, in this world, our skills became more valuable than ever. We became desired."

"Almost overnight," said Cogslow. "When we were sold into slavery —"

"Whoa, whoa — wait a minute: You're *slaves?*" asked Diana.

"Well, of course," said Bezelina. "We would never choose this life. I wanted to see my kids grow up to time reruns of *Cheers*, but now they're helping Chinese Olympians prepare for the three-meter synchronized springboard."

"A timekeeping challenge, since there's two separate divers —"

"— and since the time is largely dictated by gravity."

"That's terrible," said Maribel.

"It could be worse," said Bezelina, "they could be timekeeping for Australian archers or something."

"No, I mean it's terrible you can't see them," said Maribel. She turned to me. "Zeke, can't we just let them go?"

"That's a great, um, brainstorm," I said, "but technically, they're not our property. They belong to the company. But we can certainly utilize them more effectively? Maybe you can innovate, uh, new and agile ways of maximizing the company's stopwatch utility? In your spare time, of course."

Bezelina patted Maribel on the arm. "It's fine, Maribel, we appreciate the understanding, but this is as good a situation as we can hope for. To think — we're timing the process of creative inspiration itself!"

"A relative privilege!" agreed Cogslow.

I flashed a weak smile and shrugged my shoulders as if to say, "See, Maribel?"

"See, Maribel?" I said.

"I just feel like we're losing our way. I mean, earlier today, I was forced to inspire an article about *Game of Thrones* that said the murders of Ned and Rob Stark were powerful symbols repudiating the tyranny of white male privilege, but I thought Ned and Rob were the good guys? It's all very confusing. Plus, I'm not at all sure who it's supposed to validate. Who can take this drivel seriously while Mitch McConnell remains an absolute ghoul?" Maribel leaned her forehead against the table. "If only I'd done a better job taking over for Clara."

"Hey," said Diana, who'd been staring out the window at the many bespectacled agents sprinting back and forth across the courtyard to appear busy, "it's not your fault."

Maribel looked down. "I don't know."

"Who's Clara?" asked Cogslow. "Perhaps a Crownswellian figure?"

"Yes," said Maribel. "She led our Department during its peak creative period, from 30,000 B.C. to 2005, which is when Zeke convinced her to dumb down the script of *Crash*. But as much as we like to blame Zeke, the truth is: In the past, she would've been strong enough to withstand a *Crash*. She survived *Hustle & Hoe*, for G.'s sake. But by the mid-2000s, our work was already losing influence. *We* were losing influence. And I did nothing to stop it. I tried to reorient Inspirations around playing nicely within *THOROUGHGOOD1* but look where it's gotten us. We've become a support function. And now I fear all we're going to do is justify this miserable status quo for the rest of our eternities."

"I agree," said Diana, who'd been fuming since I empowered her to inspire some sponsored content claiming that shopping at Hobby Lobby would stop Sharia law from spreading in Oklahoma City. "It's like Brucie said. What's the G. damn point of inspiring art if the only goal is to keep people complacent? We're adapting our inspirations to fit Trent's technology but we should be doing the opposite. If we were still ourselves, we'd be interrogating what impact technology was having on humanity's moral development. Instead, we're giving them license to mindlessly consume whatever their feeds put in front of them. It's disgusting."

Worried by where this conversation was going, I reached into my pocket and clicked the remote I used to control Cogslow and Bezelina. They bolted up as though they'd been electrocuted. They began buzzing and turning red and pointing at Diana and Maribel: "Time! Time! Time! Time! Time!" they yelled. "Shame! Shame! Shame! Shame! Shame!"

"Wait a minute!" said Maribel, turning to me. "We're still on the clock?"

"I mean, obviously," I said. "This was supposed to *boost* productivity, not impede it. We're not running UNICEF here."

"I can't believe this," said Maribel.

"Ah, come on, champ... ace... How about this? We can take the ice cream to go."

Maybe it was the ice cream; maybe it was the stopwatches; maybe it was my incessant and contradictory combination of empowerment and micromanagement, but I felt Diana, Maribel, and even Brucie (who was still in the mix for some reason) growing increasingly disengaged. They were losing sight of our capital 'M' Mission to capital 'V' Validate and beginning to inspire confusing, antagonistic, and inscrutable screeds that failed to validate anyone.

"Indeed," I caught them streaming into a New York Times cultural critic, "while it may seem *discouraging*, it's actually *encouraging* that grown human beings so completely identify with music for pre-teen girls, that their political worldview stems from a combination of *Avengers* and *Game of Thrones* and *Harry Potter*, that they pound Young Adult Dystopian Sci-Fi like an alcoholic pounding Listerine in a 24-hour CVS after the bar closes. This is all wonderful, normal, and should be *encouraged*, not *discouraged*."

A more paranoid manager may have thought this tonal schizophrenia to be a veiled commentary on his management style. In some cases, the tonal shift was even more clear and abrupt.

"You know, it's possible the *Pawn Stars* are a fountain of business insight that will help you become the economic titan you were born to be...but fuck the *Pawn Stars* and every derivative thereof." Since everybody liked *Pawn Stars*, that one didn't land, but none of this went unnoticed by Trent.

"Amigo. Compadre. *Guy.* I need to level with you. Your team's numbers were never good, but now they are horrible, terrible, vomit-inducing. Bad: meet worse. Bottom: meet barrel. Chaff: meet wheat. I thought you were going to come in and *crush* this. Park: meet knock-it-out-of-the. But it seems like you're not *understanding*. Message: meet get-the. *Comprende, hermano?*"

"I think, although… Are we wheat or chaff?"

"I *thought* you were wheat, but now I'm thinking you're chaff. At the very least, your numbers have been declining for a year, which is very chaff-y. I'm beginning to wonder what's going on."

"We're trying, T.," I said. "It's been hard to motivate my — or is it our — team. They want to do good work. I know they do. But it's not happening right now. That's on me — or is it on us? I think it's on me unless it has real consequences, in which case it's on us — or maybe them. I can't remember the *Harvard Business Rev—*"

"Look, whatever the case may be, your team needs to start *delivering*, or else what am I paying you for? There are always VC-subsidized spots in my Nuevo East gig economy for agents who need clearer… dictums?"

"Ah, no! No, T.! We'll get better."

"Great! So you do *comprende*."

"Of course… Although… T.?"

"Yeah?"

"Well, if our numbers haven't changed, and humanity remains, uh, 'on the verge' — or *About To* — then is what we're doing so important? I guess I ask since… well, if we could work on *Filibuster!*, go back to how things were — just for a bit — I bet I could re-engage the team. And, I mean, there are clear, concrete ways to improve the show. I have a list, see? For example, Sonny could use a new catchphrase. 'Blackzinga!' not only alienated fans of *Big Bang Theory*, but it also wasn't clever enough to reel in people who thought they were too good for CBS's programming slate. Plus, you overlay the racial element in what has proven to be a very *not* post-racial world — I think we all misread the Obama situation — and you have a joke tailor-made to confuse and alienate. Fruit: meet low-hanging, you know what I mean?"

I could see a look of disgust creep into the corner of Trent's lips, and for a moment, I thought he would send me to the gig economy right then. But the disgust disappeared, replaced by a dead smile. "I would ask fewer questions and focus on your job."

"But I —"

"I don't know if you're cut out for the gig economy, *compadre*."

PROFIT?

I called Diana, Maribel, and (for some reason) Brucie into my office, and from my desk/ping pong table hybrid told them what Trent had said. Worried this information would demoralize them, I concluded with a speech template from *Harvard Business Review* called "Motivating Your Team Through Tough Transitions."

"Look, everyone, I know this transition has been tough. I know the work has been hard and tedious and uninspiring, but let's remember why we got into this business. To *help* people. To lift them up. Because we *believed* in G.'s vision for this sliver of the universe. Because we realized the universe's other species had it mostly figured out and so working in those other slivers would be boring. I know this work isn't what we had in mind, but right now, G. thinks its best. So... you with me?"

Maribel and Diana looked at each other, then at the ground, then at me.

"It's been hard," said Maribel, "this work is so different. It's hard doing something new after 30,000 years."

"But we can do better," said Diana, "we got this."

"Are you two kidding me?" said Brucie. "I thought our mission was to *challenge* people. To lift them up not by *pandering* to them, but by giving them the resistance they need to take off. *That's* our real mission, and G. would be wise to remember."

"Brucie, quit rabble-rousing," said Diana.

I thought I'd nailed it, but that evening, they turned in a set of openly hostile assignments that showed me I hadn't nailed a thing.

Maribel, who had been inspiring a Brooklyn-based Harvard graduate to inspire episode recaps of *The Bachelorette* for *US Weekly*, submitted this essay:

Stumbling On Class in the Bachelorette's Bourgeois Cultural Void: Season 7, Episode 3

For reality television time immemorial (seven seasons), *The Bachelorette* has posed significant problems for those who would apply a class-based reading to the political economy of the show. This statement hardly requires evidence. Season after season, we've seen a culturally, intellectually, and physically homogeneous class of agents, "the Basic Bro," fail time and again to foment any sense of collective identity. Oh, sure, they sometimes work out together, but when the roses come out, the solidarity departs faster than a creatine-induced bowel movement.

For some time, the failure of the Basic Bro to move from "class in itself" to "class for itself" perplexed scholars: Surely, the Bros must sense their structurally oppressed position. Surely, they must realize that their survival requires them to pay with dignity, and, moreover, that the system allows for no opting out: For the audience to believe in *The Bachelorette*, they need the men fighting for her to look like twats. If the men are too proud, too dignified — if they *don't* pay for their place with pride — then the show would spit them out, ending their time on television.

The initial dilemma, then, can be summed up thusly: Given all this, how could the Basic Bros *not* see that they are in natural opposition to the show's producers, executives, and that titular force of oppression herself, the bachelorette.

Of course, tremendous literature from Frankfurt and Providence has now shed light on this question, and while I would encourage you to read the original scholarship like I did during my first year studying in Boston, I summarize the reasons below:

• Sometimes, the Basic Bros actually *do* want to "get with" the bachelorette, owing to reasons as diverse as "that body is bitchin'" and "what a dime, though."

• Sometimes, the Basic Bros have deluded themselves into believing in the myth of upward mobility. A Bro might think that being on the show will help him earn sponsorship dollars from the workout supplement providers advertising on Instagram, or — if he's a truly ambitious Bro — an appearance on *The Bachelor* that will lift him into the very class that so oppresses him today.

• The most important consideration, however, is cultural: The Basic Bros genuinely believe they *aren't* embarrassing themselves — that they are *cool* for doing this. Indeed, many are *willing* pawns in this exploitative game, as they've finally found a place where they can wear tight Ts, gel their hair, and work out solely their glamour muscles without judgment. In this way, they are more akin to a religious devotee than a wage laborer: They find ABC's yoke freeing, not restrictive.

If it weren't so sad, it might be funny.

Given all of this cultural baggage, we must now flip our original premise: It's not surprising that the Basic Bros fail to develop class consciousness. What's surprising is that we could have even thought to apply a traditional materialist reading to *The Bachelorette* in the first place.

Which is why Monday's episode was so stunning.

The group date found our bachelorette, Ashley, entertaining a pack of Bros at a comedy club. She probably thought there'd be some light joking and backstage make out sessions, but our host, Chris Harrison, had a surprise for her: The Bros wouldn't be doing typical stand-up. They would be roasting Ashley.

And roast her they did.

The jokes were not jokes so much as verbal assaults, attacking her "boyish body," her lack of confidence, and her job as a dance instructor/dental assistant. At one point, Ashley cried, and not in the dignified, oppressive way of one frustrated by a surplus of suitors. For a moment, we saw what might happen — what dignity might be reclaimed — if the Basic Bros could unite against their natural oppressor.

But why? Why did this happen? Had the stultifying cultural lens suddenly lost its power? Had the scales fallen from front-runner Saul's eyes? No. Not at all. I would submit that this flash of non-squat-rack solidarity happened because *the materialist conditions of this season changed*. A running plotline of this season has been that the men *thought* the bachelorette was going to be Emily, a fan favorite from the previous season, who — to use the parlance — was a dime. However, ABC couldn't make the economics work and had to settle for Ashley. Thus, when the potentiality of a dime was supplanted by Ashley, the Bros found it easier to come together, to reclaim their dignity from the forces that would turn it into advertising time for tampons and antidepressants.

And so *this* is how we rediscover class in *The Bachelorette*. *This* is how we develop materialist possibility for reality television stars in a harsh network TV landscape. *This* is how we arrive at the hopeful question: To the extent *The Bachelorette* is a mirror for broader corporate-consumer culture, and to the extent that median middle-class incomes continue to stagnate, economic opportunity feeling less and less tangible, becoming less Emily and more Ashley, might we see a similar phenomenon unfold in society writ large? Might the 99% finally demand their fair share of the economic pie?

This episode certainly left the door open...

We just need to find ourselves a comedy club.

J.P., Ben C., and Ryan P. received roses. Bentley went home.

Diana, meanwhile, inspired the following article from a Los Angeles ad agency:

Dove's Edible Chocolate Conditioner is the New Feminist Frontier [Sponsored Content]

The commercial begins: A marginally plus-size woman gets in a shower, where she's tastefully shrouded in steam (though some cleavage and upper thigh remain visible). She's a bit down: It's been a tough (albeit dignified) day being the CFO, throwing a fundraiser for her nonprofit, going for a run by a body of water, and reading her adopted Chinese son a bedtime story.

Should I really be showering? she thinks. *Maybe I should get out and check my email.*

But then...

(Weirdly bypassing shampoo) She flips open her conditioner...

And the color comes back to the screen. (Oh, right, it has been black-and-white up till this point.)

The conditioner, which depending on your demographic info will be named Michelle (middle class), Beyoncé (upper-middle), Yemoja (upper), or "White Chocolate Alice Walton" (top .01%), begins talking in the voice of her namesake, while a song (Aretha/Beyoncé/Sade/Dave Brubeck) soundtracks.

In all formulations, the message is the same: "You are a modern queen."

Our heroine begins dancing — her emails can wait — and while her hair is being conditioned, the steam swirling around her body like an adoring crowd swirling around a stage, she tilts her head up and begins squeezing the conditioner into her mouth. *"Empowered queeeeeeeeeeeen,"* the bottle whispers.

Chris Butch, Harvard MBA and Dove's Chief Ideation Officer, is proud of his team's latest ideation: "In my mind, this is feminism's new frontier. And there's even more to do. Edible shampoo. Edible body wash. Edible toothpaste. The Asians — we'd love to get some Asian representation here so we can sell in China and Japan. Our capital 'M' Mission has just begun. We've never been ideating harder."

Given the overwhelmingly positive response to the new conditioner, it's hard to believe this empowering product ever had a near misfire. "But," Chris assures us, "it did. We thought, you know, maybe an Aunt Jemima-style syrup bottle, but that didn't play well among the social media vanguard. They really let us hear it."

As for the two or three people who believe this product exploits race and gender in garish ways, Chris had this empowering burn to dish out: "In some sense, our view was, like, 'hey, who needs quote-unquote paid mat leave when you can eat Michelle Obama, you know?' We don't want to limit women by advocating on their behalf. We want to *empower* women."

Boom! This unbiased reporter would only add one thing: Do you need some edible ointment for that burn?

————

Even Brucie, for some reason, leapt into the pool of passive-aggression when he handed me a wooden scroll called, "Barking up the Wrong Tree: Reclaiming our Neutrality in an Era of Dog v. Cat Aggression." The 20,000-word screed was a thinly veiled repudiation of imperialism — a topic I didn't know Brucie even cared about (given that he was a tree). It consisted of unbelievable digressions like this one:

Which came first: Feline pride or fawning Egyptians?

Which is to say: Did the cat sleeping in your crown get his ego from being worshipped by humans, or did his ego demand worship? If you think this is an academic question, then I am afraid you're holding back treekind.

For eons, you see, trees have been content being described as 'Majestic,' 'Stately,' 'August.' And to be fair, for eons, this was fine. We would be left alone, sometimes even honored as members of human society. On those rare occasions when a cat would dodge a canine encounter by climbing up our branches, animal control would come for the dog, firemen for the cat.

But as public budgets have been slashed, cats have begun to make their homes in our crowns with <u>impunity</u>. Majesty is worth nothing anymore. Nor is stateliness. August is the name of a damned month. If we want our neutrality back, we must <u>demand</u> it back.

So I ask again: Which came first? Feline pride? Or fawning Egyptians?

If you ever want to sleep again without a dog barking at your side, you'd be wise to answer correctly.

As I put down Brucie's scroll, I began to panic. While my/our team's work pretended to take your consumption choices seriously, it was clear Diana and Maribel were undermining Trent's vision of validation. At best, these articles would confuse; at worst, they might make you wonder whether looking to reality television and brands for socioeconomic progress was possibly insufficient.

"Are you kidding me?" I asked them, but recalling my lessons from *Crushing in a Crisis: How to Transform your Personal Economic Devastation into Subsidized Gain*, I stopped, donned a pinstripe suit, rolled up my sleeves, gelled back my hair, and added, "I'll get Benny B. on the line. You two create a plan for defraying blame to Congress. If we play this right, we can convince them that by bailing us out and paying our bonuses they'll help underwater homeowners."

"What?" asked Diana.

"Wait, no. That isn't what I meant to say. Wrong book. What I meant to say was this: *I can't believe you two.*"

Brucie coughed.

"Neither of you is acknowledging the seriousness of our situation."

Brucie jumped up and down.

"I mean, here I am, doing my best to manage us out of this dilemma, and here you are, inspiring ridiculous takes on *The Bachelor?*"

"Well, *Bachelorette*," said Maribel.

"G. dammit. I don't care. Can't you see how serious this is? Trent is planning to send us to the *gig economy*."

"What is that?"

"I don't know, but it sounds terrifying."

Brucie was now spinning around. "Look-at-me-look-at-me," he screamed, so I put him in a closet and fake-locked the door, which seemed to make him happy.

"I still don't know what the problem is," said Diana.

"Same as it ever was. I don't think people are looking for ironic Marxist readings of *The Bachelorette*. Or faux-encouraging puff pieces about Dove: Even *you* must think screeds against consumerism are tired, Diana."

"I think of it more as a screed against the cooptation of emancipatory movements by brands."

"People love brands. Trent tells me they're the only thing holding society together at this point."

"But maybe they *resent* that, Zeke."

"Even if that's true, your tone is opaque. No one who reads these will be able to tell if you're serious or making fun of them or what. This isn't some stupid and unrelatable postmodern novel, guys, this is life. *Subtlety. Doesn't. Validate.* Just tell them that they're good, politically aware people who are making the world better by watching reality television. Or that if they buy the right truck, they're good Americans who don't need to worry about homeless veterans. This isn't hard."

"I think you underestimate people," said Maribel. "If we show them why Trent's vision is wrong, why there's more to life than mere content consumption, then who knows what might happen? We're taking Trent's premise seriously — that validation is the only thing that matters anymore — but by carrying that premise through to its logical conclusion, we're showing why it's a societal and spiritual dead-end. We're using the form to undermine the form. It's beautiful."

"Absolutely zero people will get that," I said. "Everyone will just be super confused."

"Or," said Diana, "they'll be set free. Who knows?"

"G. dammit," I said, "Well, I guess we'll need to go with these since we've got no Plan B. I just pray Trent doesn't notice how un-validating they are. I must say: You bring a lot to the table, but I am not happy with how you handled this task, but also keep up the good work?"

Diana shook her head.

"Have you considered mindfulness?" I asked.

The next day, our Data Scientist called me into the new Research Department. There, he delivered a harrowing message from inside his desk/ball pit hybrid.

"This is bad, man. I don't think we've ever seen lower metrics. Some of these are negative… Negative!"

"Oh no, which metrics?" I asked.

"Metrics, man. *metrics*. Trent is going to be so pissed. And my options haven't even *begun* to vest."

"Do we know why the takes aren't landing?" I asked, though I knew the answer.

"Nah, man. We possess no insight into *why* things are happening. Just that they *are*. Then Trent comes up with a post-hoc narrative that uses the data to justify whatever he was going to do anyway. But if he sees this, we'll *all* be joining the gig economy. Ah, man, I wish I could call my mom."

"Why's that?" asked Trent, sauntering in while playing Michael Bublé's rendition of "Fly Me to the Moon" on a handheld speaker.

"Oh, nothing…" I said. "Gary and I were just talking shop. You know: metrics."

"Ah, so has Gary told you about your crappy takes yet?" asked Trent, snarling his lip as though to add, "Unlike Michael Bublé, I'm not a gentleman, so I may just *shoot* you to the moon."

"Uh… well Gary and I —"

Gary was already fleeing.

"Should we, uh?"

"Don't worry about him," said Trent. "You should be worried about you. This is the lowest readership we've ever seen. Lowest engagement we've ever seen. Lowest number of shares we've ever seen," and, as "Fly Me to the Moon" rolled into Michael Bublé's Christmas album, he added, "I'll be sending over your gig economy IDs later today. I'll need a small sample of blood from each of you."

"Wait, no! I can't let that happen. I can fix this. I promise I can fix this. I just need a day."

"I dunno. I feel like we've already invested a lot in you and we're not seeing an immediate return. We're shooting for *10X-ers*, you know what I mean?"

While this initially fanned my flaming freak-out, I realized something: I *did* know what he meant. During my management reading, I had come across the "10X Philosophy," which said you should glorify/fetishize risk-taking as a way of inspiring people to new heights. You did this by working on "10X Initiatives" — e.g., tossing terrible mortgages into CDOs and dubbing them investment grade at Goldman, shorting those same CDOs at Goldman, using public TARP money to pay out your own bonuses at Goldman, selling usurious debt to collapsing Venezuelan regimes at Goldman, doing away with capital requirements at Citi/Lehman/Morgan Stanley/Merrill Lynch, levering up and crashing the world economy at Citi/Lehman/ Morgan Stanley/Merrill Lynch, robo-signing at Wells Fargo, fraudulently charging customers for car insurance they don't need at Wells Fargo, allowing terrorists to launder money through your bank at HSBC, committing accounting fraud at Enron, committing accounting fraud at Lehman, committing accounting fraud at AIG, spinning up an unaccountable Financial Products division and crashing the world economy at AIG, duping people into defaulting on their homes in order to seize their homes and flip them for a profit at OneWest, knowingly selling shoddy mortgages to Fannie Mae and Freddie Mac at Countrywide, etc., etc. — and, in a confusing bit of imprecision, the 10X Philosophy also said that only "10X" people could work on "10X" projects, meaning you needed to eradicate 9X-and-lower employees from your organization, e.g. compliance people, auditors, your more ethical VPs.

Obviously, this philosophy could only work if your business was a monopoly, backed by deep-pocketed VCs, or "too big to fail" and therefore undergirded by taxpayer resources, but, of course, this nuance wasn't important, since, like all management concepts, 10X was less a philosophy and more a language. I threw a Hail Mary:

"Uh, totally, brah. I know. And look, brah — bro — we know we haven't 10X-ed yet, but we're *soooo* close to 10X-ing. Like, dude, we're about to 10X all over everybody here. I think the problem is our swings have been almost *too* big, you know? We've been swinging so hard we're going for like, 100X-ers, and I think if we set our sights on 10, we'll crush it."

Trent seemed taken aback: "Hmmm. You think so, brah?"

"Oh, absolutely..."

Trent frowned.

"...uh, brah."

"Well, okay. I think I can see what you're saying, bro. I'll give you a day to make this right."

———

Feeling down, I thumbed through some old inspirations — classic plays, Greek philosophy, ancient histories — hoping they could now inspire me, kind of like how a woman going through divorce consults her middle-school diary to see if her twelve-year old self can point her toward a promising new life path.

But like that woman, I was disappointed: We seemed primarily occupied with Brad's opinion of us, and who Brad was seen holding hands with, and whether Brad's hand-holding with Samantha was maybe a ruse that would precede him asking us to the dance, and Brad *not* asking us to the dance, and fuck Brad anyway, and — as "wondering what's Brad up to now" became a six-hour, vodka-fueled, FBI-level mapping of Brad's work, wife, kids, pets, and investable assets — our disappointment was tinged by past, present, and future regret.

Herodotus, in particular, was useless, as he went on and on and on about which Athenian households deserved what amount of credit for Athens's "triumphs" against the Persian Xerxes, who he went out of his way to portray as some decadent and feminine Easterner while also harping on Xerxes's fondness for the harem, which — at least by standards of masculinity in the 5th Century BCE — seemed pretty damned contradictory, especially when you consider the begging-to-be-mentioned fact that the most fearsome unit of Greek soldiers in the proverbial phalanx defending Western masculine ruggedness was the Sacred Band of Thebes, who — among other things — were gay lovers, which is, of course, 100% cool (and a 2,400-year old rebuttal of "don't ask, don't tell"): I'm just saying people can deal with a harrowing level of cognitive dissonance if it's for the home team.

Antiquity giving me nothing, I proceeded to recent modernity, but here again, I was disappointed. Reading Pynchon while listening to the Geto Boys only grew my paranoia, so like any modern human who's alone in a four-cornered room staring at therapeutic "De-Stress" candles, trying his or her damndest to ignore the creeping awareness that there is no last moment, no gathering back to home, no messenger coming from the Kingdom to fix the vessels broken at Creation, I flipped on the TV. But this was even *more* overwhelming, as the number of shows and channels and portrayals of twentysomethings making it in New York had increased exponentially, and since even sitcoms were now serialized (transforming every show into a seasons-long commitment), I didn't know where to begin. So I went to the movies, which was far simpler since the theme of every popular film seemed to be "money was awesome" (*Iron Man, Batman*) or "power was awesome" (*Superman, Mean Girls*), which was a lot of fun until I realized I had neither. For a moment I considered the radio, but music had seemed to lose entirely its dominant cultural position. I did feel empowered to do something by a TED Talk I saw, but as I thought about what that something might be, I realized the TED Talk had told me nothing of substance.

Reeling, I lay down with a sigh. An hour or so passed, giving me just enough strength to take the few steps to my window. As I zoned out, following the planets' elliptical swoops about the Sun, my mind began to wander: *I should have read one of Pynchon's shorter books, what were the non-Scarface members of the Geto Boys up to, we should have put the editorial screws on Herodotus, how long have I been at this window, how far has Neptune gone since I sat down.*

And then something happened: I laughed, as I realized this last question had — in a roundabout way — led to elliptic functions by way of elliptic integrals, and that if you squinted, my dilemma could be modeled as an elliptic function plus some huge constant, where every visible point on the plane corresponded to being either really screwed or infinitely screwed, and even if there were some theoretical way out, G. dammit if it didn't seem invisible, complex, and imaginary.

That's when I remembered the father of elliptic functions, Carl Jacobi, and his famous dictum: "Invert — always invert."

And there it was! I knew what to do. I could take the original articles, and —

Gah. No. That's not what happened.

Carl had nothing to do with this, and if I'm being honest, I didn't either. I just wanted to impress you by pretending I'd produced some profound insight, some brilliant contribution. The truth, the shameful truth, is this: I remained in bed. My curtains were drawn, my room dark as could be save for the glow of an old MacBook screen. I was procrastinating, hopping from online video to online video like I was scratching a subconscious itch, occupying the part of my brain that would once have been generating ideas. As I came to a video of a local Atlanta newsman having an on-air-seizure by way of a video of a skunk on jet skis, a thought emerged like a salmon swimming against the tide: "Did anyone even *read* our inspirations?"

I turned to my browser's search bar and input the name of Maribel's article. I scrolled to the bottom, where I found a single, solitary comment from someone called ChodeFucker77: "smdh the academy is even moralizing about bachelor now it's just a show." I stared, at first taken only by the succinctness of the argument. By the way it transformed Maribel's take into a stripped-down strawman that it proceeded to misread. But soon this lone comment, standing proudly beneath the mysterious, offensive username, made me realize something: *We'd been thinking about Validation all wrong.*

While the word connoted uplifting, "on agent's wing"-style positivity, this was an illusion of language. Connotations could be flipped, could be turned (even affirmation didn't always need to be affirmative). The audience for Maribel's take (or Diana or Brucie's) didn't need to *like* it: They could organize themselves in opposition to it. They needed a boogie man — a book to burn, a team to root against, a totem to tear down. They were — the whole world was — an army of ChodeFucker77s, waiting to be born. They just needed some Negative Validation to induce labor.

I inspired a bored Young Republican to pull up Medium.com. In big, bold letters he typed: "SMDH THE ACADEMY IS EVEN MORALIZING ABOUT *BACHELOR* NOW IT'S JUST A SHOW." While inspirees normally used an inspirational stream as a starting point, he wrote down my thoughts word-for-word. Your brains, it seemed, were slowly becoming more malleable. Worried about being derivative (a quaint concern, I now realize), I inspired him to add a subheader: "WHEN WILL THE SELF-RIGHTEOUSNESS END, AMERICA?"

Eleven sentence fragments and nineteen GIFs later, he clicked "Publish" and began sharing the post on Trent's social media platforms. I wasn't sure what to expect, but before I could worry, ChodeFucker77's plagiarized take became an immediate sensation — spreading like a virus among right-leaning content mills whose audiences had long believed that ABC's emphasis on diversity was silly, and yearned for a simpler, more traditional time when a woman could select a mate from a pack of twenty-five suitors without needing to kowtow to politically correct cultural sensitivities.

Their surprising passion for my article prompted me to inspire two additional counter-takes to capitalize on what I worried would be a temporary wave: "DOVE'S NEW PRODUCT IS AN ABANDONMENT OF AMERICA'S JUDEO-CHRISTIAN HERITAGE!" and "THESE LEAFY BASTARDS NEED TO PICK A SIDE AND THE ANSWER IS OBVIOUS: CATS."

I didn't need to worry. The wave would prove more than temporary. Nobody had read my/our team's original takes charitably (or at all), so my counter-takes landed with astounding efficacy, even (especially?) when I miscast the original argument. My counter-take against Maribel, for example, was shared millions of times, precipitating the formation of tribes, counter-tribes, and lone dudes named Terry who rallied around different pet causes: *The Bachelor's* issues with race; *The Bachelor's* reinforcement of gender tropes; *The Bachelor's* inability to produce lasting relationships; *The Bachelor's* issues with sexual assault; *The Bachelor's* not choosing Terry as a cast member even though Terry's audition tape was dope; etc. But the *real* magic was that some countered on their own, asking, "Who cares if *The Bachelor* can't produce lasting relationships?" or "Should we really entrust *The Bachelor* with a national dialogue on race?" or "Were you serious with that shit, Terry?" These, in turn, produced an accelerating, ever-escalating series of takes and counter-takes until I found I had fomented a digital form of WWI trench warfare.

The effect was immediate, or as Trent described it later, "as swift and impactful as a powerful earthquake toppling the teetering slum of a developing world autocracy." The "death count" (i.e., our numbers) 10X'd overnight, so Trent came in the following day to cheers us with champagne, claiming he'd never been serious about sending us to the gig economy, but that the looming potentiality of the gig economy was a necessary motivator to inspire our best work.

I was more nervous than ever, as I now had a secret to keep from my/our team. I couldn't let Diana or Maribel find out why their most recent articles were all of a sudden so successful. How could I? This was the first time they'd seemed happy with our new arrangement, the first time they'd been engaged in their work, the first time they didn't roll their eyes whenever they looked at me. They assumed that humanity was responding to the hidden truths they'd interleaved into their inspirations. I didn't have it in me to correct them. We'd stumbled, however unintentionally, on something *okay*. Something maybe even good. Something we could build on without having to worry about tumbling into the gig economy. Sure, it wasn't perfect, but what was?

Thus, like any relationship that's lasted thirty millennia, ours began its lying phase.

Diana, Maribel, and Brucie continued to inspire ostensibly validating but tonally sophisticated and sarcastic essays — "GIF-en Goods: How GIFs Became our Online Staple Food, and What This Portends (Hint: Irish Potato Famine)," "Why Journalism Will Be Okay (Hint: My Parents Pay for My Washington, D.C. Apartment)," "Why It's Okay All of Palo Alto's Trees Are Oaks (Hint: Meritocracy)" — that reliably sailed over the heads of the few folks who stumbled on them. (Brucie, in particular, was a surprisingly avant-garde essayist, earning star turns by proxy in *The New Yorker* and *The Paris Review of Books*, whose readers — intellectuals, academics, depressed management consultants who didn't want to admit they couldn't understand his essays — found his use of trees as a "mirror" for human society profound. His piece, "When an Oak is a Sycamore," won a Pulitzer.)

Meanwhile, I continued to inspire screeds, counter-screeds, and the occasional #TerryScreed (Terry was by now a famous social media personality, specializing in critiquing things that would be better if they starred Terry). I worked endlessly, tirelessly, stupidly to keep our rickety chariot moving — just like Noah's descendants did when they staged Elijah's ascent into heaven before murdering Elijah behind a barn.

Like Noah's descendants, we saw high and growing engagement with our illusions, and while I wish I could say we deserved our success, I had an alternative theory: As Baby Boomers retired, and their debt-laden Millennial kids graduated into an economy without jobs, everyone needed to cope. Thus, Baby Boomers tried talking to their spouses, while Millennials tried getting into prestige television. (Sometimes, there was crossover, e.g., Boomers watching make-believe prestige TV like NBC's *The Blacklist* and telling their kids "you need to check it out"; Millennials texting somebody over a dating/casual sex app and telling their parents "don't worry I think I met someone." Occasionally, there was even direct overlap, e.g., "temporary" forays into the gig economy to "pad retirement income"/ "go out and meet people"). But these aren't things that could take up all of one's time, or even a majority of one's time, or even a bit of one's time without making them crazy. And so they all did more and more online self-validation to stave off their existential disappointment.

We were dealers on a busy corner, and the good times rolled: Our numbers grew higher; people felt more validated. Violence that wasn't caused by drones, mass shootings, suicides, and opium overdoses declined. However, despite this surface-level success, I knew it was wrong. I knew it would prove unsustainable.

"So," said Maribel, strolling into my office one day, "looks like our graphs keep going 'up and to the right,' like Gary used to say. Looks like you and Trent were nervous for nothing. Ready to admit you were underestimating people?"

"Heh, yeah — maybe, Maribel," I said.

"You were so worried," she said, punching me in the arm. "But we just needed to keep *challenging* humanity. We couldn't condescend to them. Couldn't let them luxuriate in ignorance. We needed to give them what they *needed*, not what they *wanted*."

"Definitely a possibility."

"So that's why I've inspired my most challenging, important, and Straussian essay yet! This one is ostensibly about the culturally atomizing influence of cartoons, beginning with Fred Flintstone's transition from working class hero to Great Gazoo escapism, continuing to the momentarily optimistic, Bill Clinton-era collectivism of *Rugrats*, and concluding with a survey of the current wave of postmodern, post-*SpongeBob* anarcho-pessimistic 'kids shows for adults.' *But there's a twist*: The narrator is a parakeet version of the economist Joseph Stiglitz, and this is all about Henry George's land value tax."

"Sounds great, Maribel!" I said.

I looked down at my desk and waited until she left my office. When the door closed, I screamed and screamed and screamed, causing my assistant to run in and ask if I had run out of ping pong balls.

Realizing I'd become the cheating spouse who needs to commit or call it off, I went to see Trent.

"Brah. Bro. My 10X-er in Chief," he said. "What's going on?"

"Yeah, so about that, Trent. I, uh, think we may want to pump the brakes on our present set-up. I think it's great and everything, but you know: I'm not sure we comprehend the long-run ramifications of what we're doing."

"Zeke, how many times have I told you? When you join the PMC —"

"What's the PMC again?"

"The Professional-Managerial Class. Try to keep up. So like I was saying, when you join the PMC, you need to stop caring about the broader social implications of your work. I mean, you can *pretend* to care, like when you're at a cocktail party or something. But that shouldn't actually change what you do."

"Right, right… Still, it feels like maybe we should give it some time. See how it evolves, you know? With a little more information, I bet we could crush it even harder."

Trent looked away, frowning. He tapped his fingers on his desk, slowly. Just as I was beginning to get nervous, worried that my graceless reasoning had squandered whatever minimal goodwill I'd managed to build with him, he said something that surprised me: "You know, that is an *excellent* point, compadre."

"Really?"

"Really. Look, brah, I know you've been working nonstop since you got here, and I know it's been stressful. Your team should relax."

"Really?"

"Really. And, you know, I was just thinking about what you said when we first began working together again. About how you thought *Filibuster!* had potential. And I agree. I think we gave up on that too early. Maybe you should work on that for a while."

"Really?"

"Really, bro. Look, don't even trip about it. You've already 10X'd once, and I know that if we needed you to, you could 10X again. Hell, I bet you could 10X right now. You could disrupt things so hard and so fast, we wouldn't even know what hit us: We're talking cataclysmic, wide-scale disruption and devastation on a scale never before known to mankind. Extreme weather event-style disruption. Stalin labor camp-style disruption. Mass casualties, no more power, back to the Stone Age-style disruption."

"Wow… thanks, Trent, I don't know what to say."

"Don't say a thing, brah. I look forward to seeing *Filibuster! 2.* But you should take a vacay first."

We went on a year-long silent retreat to the Bamada Sector, where the Bamadans maintain an orbiting greenhouse of immense and incommunicable beauty. However, the universe being infinitely expansive, there are infinitely many such greenhouses. What makes the Bamada Greenhouse unique are the forty-one galactic poet laureates who live there, having gone crazy trying to describe it. They wander the gardens shouting inane snippets like "hummingbird / winks at / peach," "the tumbling waterfall bubbles / bumblebee," "I left him / for a lawn." Thus, you went there to see the gap between reality and the universe's most qualified descriptions thereof, not reality itself.

Having de-stressed, we began work on *Filibuster 2: MACARON MANIA*, in which Sonny Sunderson works on behalf of the macaron lobby to (again) embark on an endless filibuster, this time to (also) ensure climate change occurs so certain almond-friendly climes become waterlogged, thus ensuring the macaron lobby has a cheap supply of their water-intensive crop. Like all reboots, the premise felt at once derivative and clunky, and while I normally wouldn't have been worried about such a thing, spending so much time online had made me attuned to new possibilities. Shamefully, I logged on to see what people were saying about our pilot episode.

That's when I discovered that the arrangement of takes and counter-takes I'd set up had become the blueprint for online discourse, extending far beyond our initial *Bachelorette*/Dove/Sycamore purview and into other parts of online discussion: music, sports, politics, etc. It seemed to happen automatically, no inspiration necessary. As this culture spread, engulfing more and more of you into its toxic orbit, the counter-takes became less subtle and more simplistic, responses somehow became less charitable. In *Filibuster! 2*'s case, for example, one reviewer said, "SHOULD HAVE STAYED IN THE COMPOST HEAP: *Filibuster! 2* is Everything Wrong with the Arugula-Gargling Elite," while another said, "By Not Addressing It Immediately, *Filibuster! 2* has Implicitly Endorsed Zionism, Rendering its Climate Change Message Null and Void."

The whole thing seemed like a nightmare, but you all appeared to be enjoying it. It'd become a way to inject some riskless drama into your lives, a way to pool your collective need for self-validation into online communities ready to maintain a certain worldview, a particular ethos. Which, granted, had happened throughout your history, but now, these communities had a novel cost: To find allies in this virtual world, you needed to simplify yourself into a format compatible with Trent's software. If you remained complex, if you kept your edges, if you said, "I dunno, *Filibuster! 2* is kinda funny, right? Not great, but good," you'd find yourself trapped, a 3D blob in 2D space, unable to enmesh with your perfect, simple, 2D allies, who knew, absolutely knew, that *Filibuster* was either hot garbage or the most important show of our time.

As more and more of you accepted this Faustian bargain, a new phenomenon emerged: a virulent, weaponized strain of Talking Past Each Other.

In antiquity, TPEO would happen occasionally — in the town square, say, or during a war. But now, it had become the modus operandi of group formation, happening everywhere, always. You'd find something you could ascribe to your opponents, compress it into 2D space, and organize yourself in opposition to it, becoming, if you weren't already, 2D yourselves. Indeed, TPEO had become so validating that it was now far more important than the original takes themselves — those were mere fodder, as Negative Validation had given way to Negative Tribal Affiliation in an automatic process, impossible to arrest.

Where would this lead? I asked myself as I created a Facebook Group named "FILIBUSTER! 2 DOPE AS FUCK!!!"

———

A few months later, we were at one of Nuevo's fourteen coffee shops discussing our script for the season finale of *Filibuster! 2*, which I think suffered as we'd incorporated the internet's schizophrenic feedback, resulting in an irregular patchwork quilt of tonal shifts and thematic diversions our audience claimed we'd "left unaddressed" (our police brutality episode came out of nowhere). As we contemplated whether the ghost of Nelson Mandela should appear in a vision to Sonny (who, I should have said, was now white and being played by *Law & Order's* Dann Florek), we heard it: A shout at the end of town.

We went running, and found a scraggly, beige-uniformed agent standing next to the chain link fence that separated Nuevo East from Nuevo proper.

"COVFEEEFE. COVFEEEFE. COVFEEEEEEEEEEEFE," he screamed, again and again.

The agent was surrounded by a few guards and a number of concerned-looking Nuevo residents, who were covering their children's eyes while telling no one in particular that they had some great literature on mental illness they'd be happy to loan out.

The agent looked from face to face, continuing to scream his nonsensical call.

"Covfefe! Covfefe! Covfefe!" he said.

"Holy shit," said Diana, "I think that's Andrew — the guy who worked on *TOONY TAPIR.*"

Diana's comment caught his attention, so Andrew ran over and whispered into Diana's face: "We don't *work* on projects anymore. We *are* the projects. I'm a *NASTY GNAT* now." He pointed to a dark beige badge on his light beige jumpsuit, which featured a gnat flying up a woman's skirt (presumably to do something nasty).

While he'd been talking to Diana, I'd been trying to slink back into the crowd, but I was too late.

"YOU," he said, running up to me and poking my chest, "YOU DID THIS."

I looked around to make sure he was talking to me.

"What the hell did I do!?"

"You did this to me. *You* gave me this assignment. *You... You..."* But he couldn't figure out how to put what he was feeling into words, so he went back to screaming.

"What's he talking about?" asked Diana.

Trying to look casual, I said, "Uh, not too sure." Then, seeing a pamphlet in Andrew's pocket called "Keeping Your Sanity in the Gig

Economy," I added, "He's probably just gone crazy and he's finding someone in the crowd to ground himself. I dunno why he'd blame me for anything."

"*Blame?*" the agent said, running back to me. "Is it not *right* to blame the being who transformed us into mud-slinging automatons? Is it not *right* to blame the being who made us scale his evil model? Is it not *right* to blame the being who put me in a position to unleash this... hell... this 'covfefe' on the world? This is the worst thing I've done. This is the worst thing anyone in my position has ever done."

Trying to dodge his accusations, I ignored most of what he said (as I'd done so many times when inspiring my counter-takes to Diana, Maribel, and Brucie's work) and addressed his final point: "Hey, uh, come on champ. You'll get 'em next time. 'Covfefe' can't have been so bad, right? What was it, even? An article or something?"

He laughed. "Don't you understand? It wasn't a failure. It was the most successful tweet any *NASTY GNAT* has ever sent. And it was a damned accident. An error. A glitch. A slip of the fingers. It was my first time tweeting from the President's account and I was just supposed to send a routine statement about the fake news media. But now all these idiots, these fucking morons, are going crazy over 'covfefe.' Finding meaning in 'covfefe.' Finding damned *layers* in 'covfefe.' They're monsters, and I fear I've become one, too."

Andrew began to pace, talking at the ground. "I even giggled when it happened, you know? Thought it was funny. It's a funny word! But before I could delete it, it was too late. Different sides were claiming it as their own in-joke and having pointless digital brawls over whose in-joke it was. Some were making counter-jokes and others were penning self-serious reactions to the counter-jokes. 'THIS IS NOT NORMAL,' THEY SAID. 'THIS IS NOT NORMAL,' THEY SCREAMED INTO THE VOID. 'Covfefe' drove two days of chatter. Two *days*."

He began to sob, then whimper, then laugh. "I took this job

because it was the only one left." He dropped to his knees, pulled out a gun, and set it against his temple.

"If you go to Nuevo East," he said, "if you go to the gig economy, and you see my wife, my beautiful bride, please tell her" — and again he laughed, a dark, terrible snicker — "covfefe."

———————

The point is: I was a terrible manager.

THE GIG ECONOMY

Not long after Andrew's demise — or "whoops-ie!" as the Nuevo Daily News would have it — we hiked out to the 'I'm Feeling Lucky' button (which in Nuevo was called the 'I'm Feeling Fucked' button). We said goodbye to Brucie (who, as a tree, was barred from Nuevo East) and waited for the 'I'm Feeling Fucked' button to reboot following a firmware update.

Diana and Maribel were convinced Trent was hiding something — a hunch they'd converted into belief when the Nuevo Daily News buried Andrew's story behind a report called "ARE OUR MONKEY GUARDS WATCHING PORN ON THE JOB? WHAT THIS MEANS FOR YOUR CHILDREN'S SAFETY AKA PROPERTY VALUES."

Plus, I knew more than to protest too much, so when the 'I'm Feeling Fucked' button cheerily said, "Update complete!" we clicked, and arrived in Nuevo East.

Hmm, I thought, allowing myself a bit of hope, *it didn't seem so different.*

I mean, sure, you'd still think it was a Bangalore call center, but I had to assume the agents — bored, stressed, and beige as they seemed — were at least working on their own time and of their own misguided volition.

But then I looked up.

Every thousand feet or so, a towering, jagged crow's nest sprang up like a massive beige blast from the blowhole of a very large, very depressed whale. Their only real pizazz was a flag sporting some kind of animal mascot.

"Look," said Maribel, pointing at the flag nearest to us, "it says *NASTY GNAT*. Like on Andrew's jumpsuit."

My momentary hopefulness vanished, as I learned that the agents in these towers enjoyed privileged positions.

Chief Gnat, a gray-haired, wiry woman, looked upon her domain like Scar looked upon Mufasa before shoving him from that ledge in *Lion King*. She prowled around her nest, all the while delivering a ceaseless, rhythmic command to her beleaguered troops: "Ready... Type... Tweet! Ready... Type... Tweet! Ready... Type... Tweet!" Making me realize these humans weren't volunteers at all, but conscripts, their desperate keystrokes always one slip away from falling behind the *NASTY*, unforgiving pace.

As I staggered down the Gnats' aisle — trying, failing, and trying again to grok the scene — I saw one such slip: initially just a comma where a semicolon should have been; but then a pair of jumbled letters; then a missed word; then a whole missed tweet; then two; then three. The culprit spun around, looking wild-eyed and frantic.

"You're from Nuevo," she said. "Right?"

I nodded.

"Have you seen him? Have you seen my husband Andrew? Red hair? Probably bragging about *Jasmine v. Jafar?* He left two days ago and he hasn't come back."

She was tearing out her hair and walking away from her desk, and while a cursory glance at the room's scalps suggested the former was okay (or at least not actively discouraged), you could sense the latter was frowned upon.

The culprit's neighbor, angling his head toward his comrade while keeping his fingers moving, said, "Get back to your desk, Sam! Before she sees!"

But it was too late. Sam was too far gone. Falling to her knees, Sam looked up at the crow's nest and screamed: *"ANDREEEEEEEEW!"*

The room froze in that peculiar way that only rooms collectively willing someone to stop doing something can.

Chief Gnat glared at her provocateur from her tower. She growled and grumbled, audibly prepared to live up to her nasty name. She grabbed a big beige horn from her crow's nest and blew, summoning a deep, warlike blast that permeated her kingdom like G.'s alter ego permeated Egypt on the inaugural Passover. And although this sound didn't, you know, kill a bunch of Egyptian children, it did freeze the Gnats mid-tweet. As the interruption lengthened, as the Gnats found it possible to remove their hands from their keyboards, I could sense their fear giving way to a mix of curiosity and shameful relief — curiosity over what would happen to Sam, shameful relief as they savored their first break in G.-knows-how-long. But fear quickly reasserted itself.

Two hulking agents materialized and looked around the room, their eyes impassive. They were dressed in soothing, baby-blue jumpsuits, which might have been funny if they weren't eight feet tall, as wide as trucks, and terrifying; instead, the contrast only served to heighten their domineering, "I WILL FUCK YOU UP" ethos (which wasn't necessary, given that they had "I WILL FUCK YOU UP" neck tattoos). As they cracked their necks and knuckles in turn, the Gnats returned their hands to their keyboards, slouching in their chairs and praying to G. they would go unnoticed.

Sam was now back at her desk, sobbing, continuing to mutter to herself while cradling a picture of Andrew in her arms. One of the baby-blue brutes pointed her out. They cracked their knuckles in succession once more, grabbed her by the armpits, and dragged her away.

She looked at us and said, "I've heard there's someone named G. out there who's supposed to be in charge. You need to find him and tell him what's happening. He doesn't kn —"

But before she could finish, one of her captors bopped her on the head. Meanwhile, from her perch, Chief Gnat was making allusions to *Lion King:* "Let this be a lesson, my Gnats, in the pain and brevity of the Circle of Life!"

At this, she blew a separate, still-beige ceremonial horn that evoked the jazzy, *Captain Fantastic*-era sound of Elton John, prompting the survivors to return to their ivory prisons.

"Hakuna matata, Gnats, hakuna matata!"

"This is bananas," I said, trying to hide my panic, "Where did all of these agents even come from? This is more agents than I've ever seen."

"I guess humans have gotten pretty desperate," said Diana.

"I mean, if they're willing to live like this…" Maribel added. "They're like slaves. But why are they here? What are they doing?"

As "Hakuna Matata" began to play in the background, I wished I could take back every decision I'd ever made.

We pressed on, continuing down the figuratively twisted (but literally quite straight) aisle. As we departed from the Gnats' domain, trying and failing to incorporate what we'd seen into our view of *THOROUGHGOOD1* and the cosmos more broadly, we found ourselves dealing with the strange new dynamics of other teams.

THE FEISTY FOXES, for example, were milling around a storyboard featuring a big vat of pudding, two crudely drawn towers, and the tagline "Yoplait's Untold, Not SOOO Good Role in 9/11."

As we passed by, we heard one Fox say, "Yoplait doesn't even make pudding. This doesn't make any sense."

The agent presenting the storyboard paused and said, "You're new here. Soon, you'll realize that doesn't matter so much."

"But this is SOOO dumb, I can't imagine — wait, it worked!"

The veteran gave her a wink.

We then met *THE MANAGEMENT MOLES*, who seemed to operate in an Ayn Randian "work had better set you free or else you'll die very disappointed" milieu. Concretely, they posted to LinkedIn.

From a sociological standpoint, the *MOLES* were notable in that they seemed to be self-policing. When one agent took a break to call his wife, for example, he was promptly reported to his overseer, who gave him "constructive feedback," counted down from five, and fired him.

When a Mole named Linda died from what seemed like a combination of loneliness, exhaustion, and a sudden onset of spiritual ennui, the overseer climbed down from his crow's nest, grabbed her corpse, and dragged it atop a tiny copper-plated mole hill. He served her survivors some cake while celebrating her best submission ("SHUT UP AND GET BACK TO WORK, MILLENNIALS"). As the party wound down, the overseer shoved Linda's corpse from the mole hill, picked up the tiny copper-plated statue, and tossed it over his shoulder to the labour of eager Moles.

Next, we arrived at *THE MIRRORING MACAWS*, who included a sub-team known as *THE POLARIZING PARROTS*.

Upon first contact, I thought these two teams worked the mailroom due to the complex system of vacuum tubing delivering a ceaseless stream of content to their crow's nest overseer. The overseer, who unlike the others actually *was* a bird, would consider each bit of content as it came in, and then caw down to a pair of agents — a Macaw (who wasn't a bird) and a Parrot (who was) — with a snappy summary.

"FORMER SEC REGULATOR IN CHARGE OF OVERSEEING JP MORGAN TO TAKE JOB AT JP MORGAN," he presently squawked, prompting Agent Macaw to scurry back to his rainbow chair and remove a digital translator from his desk drawer. In a slow, careful, and dutiful way, Agent Macaw mapped one word to another until he had a new headline: "FORMER DEPARTMENT OF TRANSPORTATION OFFICIAL IN CHARGE OF HIGH-SPEED RAIL FUNDING TO TAKE JOB AT ENGINEERING FIRM BUILDING HIGH-SPEED RAIL."

The agent, now sweating — half from his weighty task, half from the Parrots keeping the thermostat set to "Jungle" — scurried back to his avian partner, who was sitting on a beige cushion, her eyelids half-closed.

When the agent delivered the two mirrored headlines, the Parrot's expression changed, her eyes going from bird-like to Bodhisattva-like. Soon, her feathers began to glow — first the reds, then the blues, then the yellows. Without flapping her wings, she ascended into the air, her feathers pointing outward like she'd been rubbed and surrounded by an invisible army of statically charged balloons.

All at once, she snapped back and fell to her cushion. "New template!" she said. "AN EXPLAINER ON ${POLITICAL_ORIENTATION} GOVERNMENT CORRUPTION AS CONVEYED BY A SINGLE ANECDOTE."

"Wow!" said Agent Macaw. "You are an artist, Patrice, a true artist. I'm going to give all these to Lawrence." The agent ran back to Chief Macaw to deliver their work while Patrice hopped off her cushion in search of worms.

Tired by the miles we'd already walked and happy to be far from the *MOLES'* depressing and self-proclaimed "#WINNING Culture," we hung around to watch a few more rounds of mirrorings and polarizations. In general, they seemed harmless: a cute puppy playing a brass instrument became a cute kitten playing a woodwind; the tyranny of pants became the slovenliness of shorts; a screed against In-N-Out became a screed against Shake Shack became a longform consideration of why coastal elites never even mention Whataburger.

"STUDENTS DEFEND CAMPUS FROM NEO-NAZI SPEAKER," Chief Macaw yelled.

Agent Macaw turned this into "STUDENT RADICALS SHUT DOWN FREE SPEECH THAT WOULD HAVE TOTALLY CHANGED THEIR MINDS," which Patrice somehow rolled into "New template! A LACK OF EMPATHY FOR YOUR ${NARROWEST_PERSONAL_SELF_IDENTIFICATION} IDENTITY IS PLACING US IN A MODERN CIVIL WAR."

"Wow!" Agent Macaw said again, and turning to me asked, "Isn't she a master? She is a master!"

"Uhhh…" I said.

Diana jumped in: "Shouldn't we maybe avoid using an expression like *Civil War* so casually?"

The agent — who'd already started translating the headline "JOHN OLIVER CARPET BOMBS MYTHICAL WAR ON CHRISTMAS" to "JOHN OLIVER CARPET BOMBS CHRISTMAS" to "STUPID WAR ON CHRISTMAS CROWD THINKS JOHN OLIVER CARPET BOMBED THEM" — frowned. "I don't follow," he said.

"I mean, at best, it feels dramatic, and at worst, it feels self-fulfilling. I mean, look, I love producing extreme art as much as the next agent. The whole Existentialist movement was a product of a few bad months I was having romantically. But I can't see the value in this. If people *think* there's a civil war, they'll begin to *behave* like there's a civil war."

"Ehhh," said Patrice, who'd waddled over from her lunch. "This group of humans is the least violent group of humans ever. But they're also the most easily *bored*. If we don't spice up this callaloo, they'll lose interest, they'll lose focus, and then they may end *up* in a civil war. Trust me, girl, this is a replacement for violence, not a precursor."

"With all due respect," said Maribel, "this seems like dangerous reasoning. I mean, it may be true *now*, but it seems like over time, such rhetoric —"

"Are you really a parrot?" I blurted out.

Patrice glared at me, then Maribel, then me again. "I *wasn't* a parrot until I started doing this job. I volunteered for the transformation so I could get a 7% raise. Most of my colleagues choose to stay human even if it caps their upside... You know what? Screw this." Patrice cawed and flew away, muttering, "I can't be dealing with this nonsense today. G. damned Inspiration, Inc., think they know everything. Just because he came up with the system thinks he can talk down to me for being a parrot."

"I get it," Maribel said to Agent Macaw, "well, aside from being a parrot. I just think we should reserve words like carpet bombing and civil war for actual carpet bombings and actual civil wars, or else these things lose their meaning. Plus, I can't imagine you're getting permits for these kinds of claims, right? Even when Diana pitched Clara on Existentialism, she could only justify it by filing a permit arguing it would be an improvement over nihilism."

You know," the agent said, "sometimes I feel the same way. The other day I had to say that Wisconsin cheese subsidies were a kind of nuclear holocaust on the global cheese trade for the Wall Street Journal opinion section."

"It's not so bad, though, right?" I said. "Like, people don't take it literally?"

"Oh, no, they do. That was our most shared cheese-related article ever."

I began chewing on my fingernails: "So did anything good happen?"

"Well, it was our most shared cheese-related article ever."

"And that's it?"

"I guess… I mean, what did you expect it to do?"

"I dunno — maybe convince people to not have cheese subsidies?"

"Ha!" the agent said. "No, no, I mean, our next article was '9 Ways Wisconsin Cheese Subsidies Boost American Security, You Piss-Drinking Communist [Sponsored Content],' and it went on from there."

I began to hyperventilate. Realizing hanging out in this area was too risky, I grabbed Diana and Maribel by the shoulders and told them we should keep going. As we were leaving, Chief Macaw saw us and yelled down: "We perfected your system, wouldn't you say?"

When I didn't respond, he kept going: "I mean, we took your system and scaled it a million billion times. Once Patrice develops a template, we can feed it to Trent's AI and then — *boom* — infinite content! A 'thank you' would be nice."

"Come on," I said, pulling Diana and Maribel's arms harder.

When we were further along, Diana asked, "What the hell was he talking about?"

"Uh, I mean, who knows? He's a bird, right? Plus, I'm sure none of this is making its way into the world anyway," I lied. "Maribel said it herself: this is all unpermitted."

We heard a faint shout from Patrice: "New Template! ${POINTLESSLY_CONTROVERSIAL_CELEBRITY}{OWNS HER HATERS | TAKES A DUMP ON AMERICA'S CHEST} BY TWEETING ${SOMETHING_INCREDIBLY_BANAL}."

"What was the *system* he helped you scale?"

"I don't know! This is all nonsense! Maybe we should just go back to Nuevo and regroup. Hakuna Matata, you know. A problem-free philosophy."

Diana squinted at me.

"No," said Maribel, "there's more to this floor. We have to find out what."

So again we pressed on, passing a flurry of teams with bizarre, confusing, and esoteric goals.

THE JERKY JELLYFISH, for example, glided into comment threads so they could stir up jerky drama, e.g., by posing as conservative uncles and ridiculing their college-aged nephews' Bernie Sanders Facebook reposts. *THE ELEVATING ELEPHANTS*, meanwhile, had the ostensibly nobler aim of choosing people and things to trumpet in dramatic fashion, including *Hamilton,* the cast of *Hamilton,* the creator of *Hamilton,* the *Hamilton* soundtrack, single mothers who'd taken out second mortgages so they could get their kids tickets to *Hamilton,* and that time the *Hamilton* cast — at tremendous personal cost — challenged their audience by behooving a Republican Vice President to consider diversity. In a strange symbiosis, *THE BACKLASH BEARS* would drag those same people and things back down upon waking from their increasingly abbreviated hibernations (although they seemed to be having a hard time mounting an assault on *Hamilton*). The *BEARS* encompassed a sub-team known as *THE*

REFRACTING RHINOS, which specialized in turning affirmative movements — women arguing for representation in the video game industry, say, or Black Americans pointing out problems with policing — into sinister totems that preteen boys and NFL fans could charge, furiously, again and again. Meanwhile, *THE CENSORIOUS CENTIPEDES* bypassed the Elephant/Bear-and-Rhino back-and-forth altogether by finding helpless, hapless people to destroy under a many-legged stampede of outrage, whether it was people who donated to certain political causes, people who tweeted misunderstood jokes, or people who were insufficiently outraged at people who donated to certain political causes or tweeted misunderstood jokes.

It felt like walking through a sadder, beiger coral reef, a point whose poetic resonance became clear when we arrived at the floor's final team: *THE FRAUDULENT PHYTOPLANKTON.*

From far away, the *PLANKTON* seemed to be doing nothing at all, looking as lifeless and sedentary as a knowledge economy worker who's just eaten a carb-y lunch. As we came closer, however, we could hear faint, frantic mouse clicks, which grew in sound and fury as we crossed the dark beige threshold and entered the phytoplanktonic domain. The thick smell of BO that accumulates when teenage boys play video games for too long hung heavy, as sweaty temples and even sweatier armpits had been neglected for internet eons.

I looked at their screens to figure out what could be commanding such focus, but the planktonic movements seemed erratic, random, like they were responding to stimuli only they could see. Eventually, I did discern a pattern: the intensity of their movements seemed to bare some relation to a big graph hanging from the team's crow's nest. When the line in the graph fell, the clicking grew more urgent; when the line in the graph increased, the clicking grew more measured.

Three towering chrome letters hovered above the graph: "R.O.I."

This information told me nothing about what the clicking or the graph represented, so while I felt bad about interrupting — and indeed, almost felt like I'd be interrupting something sacred, like a Catholic grandmother doing the rosary or an Olympic luger preparing to luge off — I was even more curious. I made a motion to tap an agent on the shoulder, but before I could follow through, I heard a call: *"ARE YOU CRAZY?!"*

We looked up to find who the voice belonged to and saw Chief Phyto clambering down from his crow's nest in a panic. He sprinted toward us, worried I would go through with my plan to tap his agent's shoulder.

"Are you crazy?" he asked again when he arrived, winded from his dash. "You can't just — wait, WHOA."

He dropped to his knees.

"It's you!" he said.

"Uh, it's me?"

"Wow," he said, eyes bugging out, "what an honor. To think: *I* was going to reprimand *you*. Of *course* you know this is a delicate ecosystem. Of *course* you know that if he doesn't click, then all of this — everything — this whole damned floor — falls apart."

"I think you have me confused with somebody else," I said.

"No, no, it's you! You made all this work! You're the reason return on advertising investment is higher than it's ever been!"

"What's he talking about?" said Maribel.

"Oh, man, all *three* of you made this work. I'm DeMar, by the way. Wow! Wait till I tell my wife I met you today. She's going to be blown away."

"*Why* is she going to be blown away?" said Diana.

"*You* made this all work. *You* saved the whole operation. For the longest time, the only ads we could run profitability were for penis enlargement —"

"So you do advertis —"

"— but then you realized: 'Hey, every take is a counter-take waiting to be written, and every counter-take can — if done well — be a reflection of someone's identity.'"

"Could you back up —"

"And what underlies advertising? *Identity. Demographics.* You had to chop people up like a market research firm, and then you had to remind people — every single minute of every single day — what segment they belonged to. *That's why we can sell niche products like never before:* Shaving kits for men who read 'HOW TO BE A MAN' content. On-demand Latin tutoring for parents who read 'HOW TO KEEP YOUR KID OUT OF THE GIG ECONOMY' content. Serious mobile games for guys who read 'HOW GAMING HAS BECOME POLITICALLY CORRECT' content. All things that are maybe — if you squint — maybe kind of useful? All things that you would only *BUY*, however, if you were thinking of yourself as a manly man/competitive parent/serious gamer. Just like the only time someone buys penis enlargement pills is when he's watching porn and feeling underendowed. Don't you see? What am I talking about? Of *course* you see. It's all connected — all, when you think about it, a kind of penis enlargement ad. Brilliant, brilliant, *brilliant.*"

"I dunno if I'd call it brill —" I began.

"But it's not so simple — no, your brilliance runs deeper!"

"Thanks, but you can stop —"

"There were *always* niche groups online. But they were *spread out.* In blogs. Chat rooms. *Communities.* The gamer never *met* his feminist bogeywoman. He just ranked *Final Fantasy* heroines by hotness alongside his community of virtual pals. No way you could run any serious ads in that kind of place. *Not unless you helped him realize his economic potential.* So you and T. needed to bring all of these communities *together,* onto centralized platforms: Facebook. Twitter. YouTube. Then our gamer friend *would* meet his feminist bogeywoman. *Would* feel embattled. *Would* feel under siege. And so would everyone else! Because we could bottle up that feeling and ensure every piece of content we made was *steeped* in it. What could be better? *THREAT IS THE PERFECT CATALYST FOR GROUP FORMATION, AND GROUPS ARE THE PERFECT TARGETS*

FOR HYPER-OPTIMIZED ADVERTISEMENTS. Thus, the casual gamer becomes the serious gamer becomes the *INSATIABLE AND ANTAGONISTIC CONSUMER!"*

"Please, please stop —"

"And, of course, there's an irony to all of this: Even though humanity is more geographically sorted than ever before; even though their real-world communities are more ideologically and culturally homogenous than ever before; even though they're no longer marrying across class lines or educational lines or political lines; you've made their baboon brains think the opposite! They think they're all fighting over the same damned mountain! IT'S AN ADVERTISING BONANZA."

I'd been motioning him to stop, but DeMar was too excited.

"I'll be honest, when you inspired that response to Maribel's *Bachelorette* recap, I thought it was stupid. Why would anyone have such a strong reaction to a *Bachelorette* recap? But then I saw how much easier it was to advertise. We could sell *Bachelor* brand Tummy Tea to people who'd been confused by the exchange; *New Yorker* subscriptions to people who thought they were too good for the exchange; home security to people who agreed that the academy was ruining America; 3D printed Terry dolls to Terry."

"What are you talking about?" said Maribel.

"*You* inspired *Stumbling On Class in the The Bachelorette's Bourgeois Cultural Void: Season 7, Episode 3*... and *he* inspired *SMDH THE ACADEMY IS EVEN MORALIZING ABOUT BACHELOR NOW IT'S JUST A SHOW.* That was the blueprint. That's how our whole floor works now, and we can sell ads, *ads*, ADS like never before. WE ARE PRINTING MONEY."

"WHAT?" said Maribel.

"YOU FUCKING BASTARD," said Diana, turning to me.

"WE WERE PROTESTING WHAT WAS HAPPENING AND YOU TURNED IT INTO... PORNAGRAPHY."

"I can explain," I said. "Trent would have —"

"No. FUCK YOU A THOUSAND TIMES," said Diana, and — flipping me off with both hands — flew away in reverse.

Maribel shook her head and followed.

I dropped to my knees.

DeMar was so starstruck that he didn't seem to understand what was going on. "And man… I have to say… the way you solved this by applying G.'s s parable. Unbelievable. Everyone on this floor always talks up Patrice, but *you* are the real master."

I looked up at DeMar and asked, "What do you mean?"

"THIS GUY," he said.

"Seriously, what do you mean?"

He looked confused: "The Tower of Babel, right? You turned humanity's biggest achievement into the Tower of Babel."

PART 2:
Earth

LOST

I fell through space, tumbling toward Earth, alone.

I wish I could say I had a plan, but the truth was I had nothing else to do. I had no power. Could mount no struggle. I had become, embarrassingly, a cliché, a fallen angel, passing through the Solar System to hover impotently above New Zealand. Unable to think and unable to land, I began circling the world.

From above, your planet looked so calm, its many youthful indiscretions (volcanism, glaciation, methane hydrate gasification) long gone, calcified into mountains surrounded by clouds of kindness: "Nothing amiss down here, governor!" your planet seemed to say.

Of course, I knew this sentiment was a lie, an illusion which, contra gravity, grew more powerful with distance — and, boy, had I been distant.

In the old days of *THOROUGHGOOD1,* we would consciously ward off this illusion, remind ourselves it wasn't there. We knew that if we didn't, we would inevitably succumb to that most beguiling of bureaucratic inclinations: the tendency to turn inward. Our work would become an end instead of a means. Our colleagues would cease to be teammates with a shared goal and become rivals, antagonists, belligerents engaged in petty feuds over pornography and dog breeding and opium.

In a moment of shame, I see that your planet's clouds of kindness are nothing but CO_2 pouring into its atmosphere. That's when I realize: I hadn't actually *been* to your planet in years. Even from the stratosphere, I could see how much had changed: Venice was all cruise ships now; Southeast Asia was all lit up; China was all trains and skyscrapers. And while I'd known all of this cerebrally, none of it had seeped into my intuition. Why the hell was I going on about Genghis Khan when you'd clearly moved past him? Beijing and Inner Mongolia were joined by a *high-speed rail* now. 'Shut up, guy!' you must've been yelling. Meanwhile, the world's most historic cities — London, Athens, uh, Atlanta — were being marred by decaying, publicly-funded markers of illicit Olympic excess and the only thing I could think to do was reboot *Filibuster!?*

You know, I thought, *maybe it was simple. Maybe the reason I'd returned was so I could go back down. So I could reengage. So I could reconnect. Maybe the reason I'd come back was so I could become a damned agent again.*

Feeling renewed, I closed my eyes and plunged through the atmosphere...

———

When I was through, I opened my eyes and took in an eternity-af-firming view of the rugged California coastline. Still beautiful, but a touch more meager, sanded down by the relentless, unyielding, and erosive Pacific, which — when combined with the state's unfunded pension liability and the ruinous consequences of Prop 13 — could form the backbone of a compelling John McPhee book named maybe *Disassembling California* (although someone will need to pass that on to John: he's refused any attempts we've made to inspire him).

I passed the Port of Long Beach, where I saw goods coming in, goods going out, and the occasional cruise ship bearing Orange County teenagers to Mexico for their high school graduation trips. I saw lines of people outside Disneyland, lines of cars on the 405, and lines of crops in Fresno. When I flew over San Jose, I got a glimpse of the house where one of my old focus group couples, Luis and Mari, used to live. The last time I'd been there, I'd been doing research on behalf of Clara. I told the couple about a new show idea she was workshopping and asked them if we should set the show in San Jose. To my surprise, they said, "Oh, no. San Jose is too boring." Which is how the *Friends* ended up living in a huge New York City apartment that would have at least made sense in 1990s San Jose.

I flew over San Mateo, Burlingame, San Bruno. When I arrived at 380, I cut west — west to P-Town, where another of my old focus group members lived. Pacifica was the blue-collar pantry to San Francisco's Sur La Table kitchenette. A place where plumbers lived so the people in Pacific Heights could have their toilets fixed without running the risk of seeing their plumbers about town in a non-plumber capacity.

The member of my focus group was named Karen, and she was someone I'd missed, someone I hoped could snap me from my funk. She'd always had the power to intuit what humanity needed, so I believed she could now help me save you (and there was precedent, as she'd saved *National Treasure 9: Martha Washington's Crotchless Panties* when she made us remove the ill-advised scene in which the Aaron Burr-Alexander Hamilton duel is reimagined as an elaborate BDSM ritual).

I suppose I should explain how Karen and I came to know each other.

If I were being blunt, adhering fully and completely to *TG1: Standards & Practices*, I would say this: our focus group needed a widow.

If I were being less blunt — if I were, G. literally forbid, showing one of you some unpermitted empathy — I might say that Karen had a husband, George, but that George passed away in an industrial accident. I might explain how the accident happened in the Dogpatch, close to where the San Francisco Giants play baseball today. I suppose I would explain how Karen donated half of the settlement money to her church, and with the other half built a house overlooking the strip of beach she and George walked along every Sunday, and I would add that she continued to do the same walk, every week, as a way of being with him. I would probably explain that she was miserable, but eventually she was sometimes happy. She'd always wanted to live by the beach.

Assuming I went into so much detail, I think I'd need to say that when she built her house, it was forty feet from the bluff, but the P-Town fog consumed the bluff bit by bit, morning by morning, until forty feet became thirty feet and thirty feet became twenty feet and twenty feet became ten feet. I would also have to add that the moment she built her house, I could see this would happen, which would naturally require some answer, e.g., perhaps I filed a permit application with the Department of Natural Disasters to slow the fog's erosive impact, but I got back a form letter saying a one-woman incident fell outside their purview so would I please convert the property to a hotel and refile or try the Department of Miraculous Interventions next time.

Now, perhaps still feeling guilty, I flew down to Karen's new home, which she'd moved into when her old living room tumbled into the sea.

P-TOWN

A pamphlet fell from the porch awning and hit me in the face.

"LEAVE NOW," it said, "I WILL STAND MY GROUND." (This warning was accompanied by a picture of Paul Revere, who was, of course, famous for *not* standing his ground, but I digress.) When it became clear I wouldn't leave, a grinding thump issued from inside, as though somebody were dragging open a submarine door. After a few more pamphlets (James "I AM G. DAMNED SERIOUS" Madison; Andrew "I WILL SKIN YOU ALIVE" Jackson), a peephole on the porch door slid open, straining against years of grime like a blunt knife through a fancy cheese. From the pungent void, a pair of wild eyes shone dimly, pupils shrinking and dilating and shrinking again as recognition fought through fear, confusion, and — as I would soon learn — rage.

A voice, intermingling with the smell, said, "Zeke? Is that you?"

"Yes, Karen," I said. "I'm — I'm sorry it's been so long. I had to live in New York for *Friends*, see, and there was a lot of buzz about a spinoff, and —"

The peephole snapped shut, leaving my excuse dangling.

I stood alone and confused in the P-Town breeze.

Moments passed.

More moments passed.

A seagull landed on the railing and looked at me as if to say, "Why are you hanging out here like a doof, you dumb doof?"

Thinking this seabird had a point, I began to formulate a Plan B. Perhaps I could drop in on Luis and Mari. They *had* been right about *Friends*, but San Jose was so boring…

Before I could complete my thought, an alarm sounded and Karen's porchlights turned an ominous green. Glass walls sprung from the planter boxes bracketing the porch, encasing my gull friend and me in a glass bubble that reminded me of a tinier t-Dome. Red gas was piped into the dome, killing the seagull promptly (who's the doof now?), while a computer voice ripped from a 90s movie spoke over the sound of the alarm:

"Do not be scared, friend. You are being purified in the cleansing fumes of the JOHNBIRCHBOX. You may feel yourself losing consciousness. Do not be scared, friend. This is normal. If you remain unconscious for more than four hours, please consult your doctor. By acknowledging this safety message, you waive your right to legal recourse. Thank you, friend, on behalf of all of us here at MONBLACK."

"A Monsanto/Blackwater JV," the voice added in a form of verbal small print.

When the safety message and gassing were over, the alarm went quiet and the porchlights returned to a standard porchlight yellow. As the dome collapsed into the planter boxes, Karen's door swung open. Her frail white figure streamed toward me like a ghost.

"Quick," she said, pulling me by the arm, "Get in now. *Before they see.*"

She slammed the porch door behind me and reinforced it with the large metal door I'd heard earlier. Surprisingly spry for a woman her age, she sprinted to a keypad and punched in a code, prompting the computer voice to return.

"Your home is now being secured by SAFESPACE, a MON-BLACK security system and proud corporate sponsor of the 2nd Amendment."

I began to say something, but the computer voice cut me off: "Let's see those snowflakes get in now, eh, Karen?"

Overcome by questions and overwhelmed by the in-your-face branding of Karen's home security products, I couldn't speak. Eventually, I spit something out: "What the *hell* is going on, Karen?"

Karen wasn't responding. Mumbling half to me, half to herself, she said, "Zeke, I thought they got you I thought they got you Zeke, you working in the movie business so exposed so exposed right there in the open so happy to see you Zeke, I'm sorry I had to detox you I thought I would need to vaporize you but detox seemed to work my goodness Zeke it's been so long."

"Uh, right, but—"

"And Zeke things are so bad Zeke they've never been worse. Carnage riots sanctuary cities open borders it's carnage Zeke it's all carnage."

"It can't be *so* bad, Karen — I mean, we're together again."

This sentiment seemed to calm her, so I continued: "It's so good to see you — you have no idea. *I've missed you*, Karen. And, wow, look, you've done some wonderful things with the place. That is a lovely, ah, a lovely —"

I looked around, trying to find something I could compliment, but this was hard since Karen's home was dark, extremely dark, its distinguishing characteristics open pill bottles; four TVs all, for some reason, set to the same channel; and a digital map of the Bay Area named "BAYWATCH by MONBLACK," which purported to show you — on the basis of social media sentiment analysis — a real-time assessment of "geographic threat," which was Orange everywhere but Red in Berkeley and San Francisco, which the map referred to as "Bezerkeley" and "San Fran Sicko."

"— is that a *cage?*"

"Thank you, Zeke."

She was scribbling furiously into a notebook. "What are you doing?" I asked.

"Some freelance gerrymandering."

"Wait, why?"

"Ha! Isn't it *obvious*? A Latin couple just moved in down the street so I'm redrawing our district to be safe."

"Karen. That's insane."

"This is *politics*, Zeke. It's us or the neo-Marxists."

"I dunno, Karen, I'm not sure neo-Marxists have a real constituency in Pacifica, or, like, anywhere. I've been traveling—"

"Traveling?"

"Yeah, outside, and—"

"Out-side? Zeke, are you insane? Look at this map — we are on the verge of being *overrun*."

"Overrun by *who*, Karen?"

"Don't be cute, Zeke, you and I know both know we have no time for that."

"You know, maybe we should take these pills here and revisit some assumptions—"

"Pills? Now you're being silly. You know just as well as I that they're mind control devices made by the Deep State Department."

"I don't think that's true at all, Karen. Indeed…"

But then I looked around — and I mean *really* looked around: The untaken pills were for Alzheimer's, and the TVs were streaming a continuous loop of big-haired newsmen with names like Tucker Peterson and Peter Tuckerson and P.T. Tuckerpete, who mostly seemed to fear monger about topics they confusingly regarded as both impotent and terrifying: "THE UN!" "THE EU!" THE HOLLYWOOD ELITE!" But occasionally they would stop to hawk gold or guns, sometimes even combining the two, as I learned when I saw Karen dialing a number for a gold-plated gun called THE DEFLATOR.

"Whoa whoa whoa, Karen — why would you need that?"

"Another zinger, Zeke. I have Amazon Prime."

"I'm not sure I follow—"

"But, for now, you can use this," she said, tossing me a rifle she'd grabbed from her pantry.

"I'm good, thank you anyway," I said, placing the gun on the chair behind me.

"You're serious?"

"Yeah — I mean, I flew up from L.A. just now, and it was cool. Way easier than usual."

"G. dammit, Zeke. You got out of L.A. alive? I thought it had already fallen."

"Fallen to *what*, Karen?"

"Fallen, Zeke, fallen! *We* are the last bastion."

"We *who*?"

"We *Pacifica*. According to my research, everywhere — *everywhere* else — has been taken over."

"G. dammit, Karen — by *who*?"

"By… them," she said, pointing a shaky finger toward the Facebook Feed on her phone.

I looked at her screen and saw nothing but… memes.

Well, memes and ads. Ads and memes. Memes. Ads. Memes. Ads. As far as my finger could scroll.

I could see in this content the handiwork of my spiritual successors in Nuevo East. The paradoxically named *O-Bambi's ACA Death Squads*, for example, showed a swarthy O.J. Simpson sentencing a grandma to die on Christmas. (The accompanying ad was for a form of Death Squad life insurance: "A wonderful **Christ**mas gift," the ad said.) Meanwhile, the depressingly clichéd *O-Bambi's Sanctuary* showed an idyllic Virginia town overrun by drug gangs with a call to "Caption This!" leading to comments that ranged in creativity from "Aye aye aye — we take your health care" to "Social Security, por favor?" (The accompanying ad was for SAFESPACE by MONBLACK: "Don't let MS-XIII take *your* Medicare," the ad said.) Finally, and in somehow even poorer taste, *O-Bambi's Kenyan Gun Theft* listed every mass shooting that couldn't be blamed on ISIS, tagged the family members of the slain, and called them "ANTI-2nd AMENDMENT FALSE FLAG SOROS MONKEYS." (The accompanying ad was for THE DEFLATOR, and it was personalized, since it said, "Reign in the forthcoming fall of fiat currency with your second DEFLATOR of the day, Karen!")

"Holy shit, Karen. You realize O-Bambi — I mean, Obama — isn't even the President —"

"Yes, Zeke, *yes*. You get it. The college kids — bought and paid for by Angelina Jolie and Colin Kaepernick — are ruining America by *trampling on free speech*."

"I'm still not sure I follow—"

"WELL-ACTUALLY!" something croaked, causing me to spin around in a panic.

"What the hell is that, Karen? Did somebody say something!?"

Now that my eyes had acclimated to the dark, I could see a shadow moving in the cage I'd complimented previously: "HOLY SHIT, KAREN, IS THERE SOMEONE IN THAT CAGE?"

The shadow moved, climbing upward by supporting itself on the bars of the cage. It slid into the blue glow of Carl Tuckerson's segment, "ANTIFA'S WAR ON CHRISTMAS."

I could see now that the shadow was a once-handsome man who'd grown shabby, smelly, and haggard in his weeks (months? years?) of captivity.

"Well-actually," he said again, coughing erratically, "strictly speaking, that isn't true. For one, broad-based campus attitudes toward free speech haven't changed by nearly as much the narrative surrounding them has. Indeed, what we see on campus mimics what we see in society writ large, where a small, hyperpolarized group enjoys outsized influence for a complex array of interrelated reasons that would be hard to summarize from this cage I'm in. This is not to make some normative claim about this *particular* group, or any other. As food for thought, Civil Rights began as a small-scale movement, and it would never have had the impact it did were its adherents *not* hyperpolarized, *not* sure of the moral righteousness of their cause, *not* capable of confidently exposing society's injustices. However, we should be aware that the *same* dynamics that lead to powerful movements for Civil Rights or Same Sex Marriage can also lead to more sinister developments.

The alt-right, for example, can in some sense be seen—"

Karen zapped him with a taser. He cried out and fell to the ground, convulsing on the "fakenewspaper" (Karen's expression) lining his cage.

"PolitiFact Reporter," she said, "in the '*Corrections*' business." She spat and zapped him again.

"G. dammit, Karen, you need to let this guy go."

"To rejoin his Maoist Machine?"

"You have to."

"I can't."

"The *old* Karen would let him go—"

"HE KNOWS TOO MUCH, ZEKE. HE CAN SABOTAGE EVERYTHING."

"The world isn't as bad as you think." I said, straining to think of an example. "Like… You know how Mongolia and China were always sniping at each other? Well, they're connected by a high-speed rail now, and their standard of living—"

Karen laughed. "The world isn't as bad as I think," she repeated, laughing harder, filling the room with a new kind of darkness. "My husband died for a job that doesn't exist anymore, and do you know what replaced his factory, Zeke? A high-end cocktail lounge *slash* bowling alley. The developer tore out the memorial plaque his union put up to honor him and didn't even send it to me. The lanes cost $45 an hour."

"I'm sorry, Karen, I—"

"But, oh, thank G., thank G. I can take solace in my church, right? Wrong, Zeke. It had to shut down because nobody went anymore. All my friends in the congregation moved to Sacramento because they couldn't afford it here. Plus, I have a feeling, though I can't prove it, that my priest stole the money I donated. He's in Italy now on 'Special Assignment.'"

"Truth Score… 98%," the PolitiFact Reporter said, trembling from his earlier shocks.

"Shut up, you!" she yelled.

"Okay, okay," I said, and — trying a new tack — continued: "I'm sorry, Karen. You're right. Things aren't great. They're crappy. That's why I'm here. I was hoping we could work together to fix things, somehow. But then you were sad, and I was just trying to cheer you up. You can forgive me for trying to cheer you up, can't you?"

For the first time, she smiled, and I almost thought I could see her eyes twinkling. "Well, yes. I suppose I can forgive you for that."

But this moment, this possible launching pad of connection, ended, interrupted by a sound from Karen's phone. She looked down, frowned, and her eyes dimmed once again. "Look, Zeke," she said, "you don't know how horrible it is out there. Look at my phone."

So I did, and saw ping upon ping upon ping — each one a drip from an IV, each a short-circuiting of Karen's brain:

PING: "Sports anchor criticizes President!"

PING: "Football players kneel!"

PING: "College students shout down fringe podcast host!"

"These don't seem like real problems," I began, but it was too late — she was engrossed...

That's when I knew: There would be no winning. No way to combat the digital flood. By the time we'd discussed one ping, a thousand more would sprout like weeds, weaving a JOHNBIRCHBOX so thick and impenetrable that Karen would never escape. Still, I found myself making one final, futile plea: "Surely, these are exaggerations, Karen. I was just, uh, traveling, and things really did seem okay."

"You aren't seeing things from my perspective," she said.

I realized that she was right. I hadn't been, but I *could* be.

Clearing my mind, I became an emotional radio, ready to tune into Karen's unique frequency. When I found it, I moved closer and closer, not all at once, but like a top spinning from one side of a coffee table to another, gracefully and carefully, sometimes moving straight, sometimes moving in a circle, sometimes even moving backwards, trying to keep my head while I dipped into someone else's. The last time I'd done this, I'd been gauging someone's disbelief at Jennifer Aniston going for David Schwimmer on *Friends*, which is to say: I was rusty. This wasn't quite so simple as riding a bike.

Thus, even though I'd been careful, I felt overwhelmed by the flood of foreign emotion: *Anger about which shows were popular. Confusion about why people seemed to hate cops. Fear about healthcare budgets. Sadness about my nephew's son, who called me "grams," never calling, never even liking my Facebook posts even though I could see his little green icon was always on. The nerve! Some of my posts had even been olive branches! My tryptic on "All Lives Matter," for example, seemed like it could have reeled him in, but it's like he didn't even read it...Oh, no. Oh, G...Do you think he could have muted me? Well, we'll see how he likes it when I tell him I'm not paying his tuition anymore...*

Sensing an in, I lowered the emotional volume and asked, "How's your grandson Kevin doing?"

"Oh, you mean Chairman Mao, Jr.? Couldn't tell you. He never calls. Never even messages me on Facebook."

"I mean, he's in college, right? He could be busy?"

"Busy. Busy, busy, busy. Too busy for his grandma, that's for sure. He's studying at some college in the East Bay, which according to my research has been taken over," she said, motioning toward BAYWATCH, "so who knows."

"We should go see him. We can go together so it's not scary, and then I can show you that your map is wrong. Kevin is doing fine, and I'm sure he'll be happy to see you."

But Karen was done.

She mumbled something about being sleepy and walked into her TV room, where she plugged her phone into what looked like a burgundy massage chair. She sat down and pulled the chair's accompanying helmet onto her head, and the helmet flashed as it translated the pings from her phone into powerful cranial shocks. Karen spasmed and went numb. Meanwhile, the PolitiFact Reporter, having recovered from his own shock therapy, was busy fact-checking the lies emanating from Karen's TV.

"WELL-ACTUALLY, it's not true that…"

"WELL-ACTUALLY, it's not the case that…"

"WELL-ACTUALLY, it's misleading to say that…"

When her electroshock therapy was finished, Karen got up, walked over to the PolitiFact Reporter, and zapped him — again and again and again.

"Thank you for choosing EXECUTIVE ORDER!" the computer voice said. "The same great tech we've been using to lobotomize US Presidents and Middle Eastern Strongmen since 1969… now available from the comfort of your own home!"

BEZERKLEY (OR IS IT?)

On the bus ride to Berkeley, I developed a plan: Find Kevin; bring him home to Karen; they would have a lovely dinner; things would be okay, somehow. Sure, it was formulaic, but in trying times such as these, do we not become more, rather than less, susceptible to fantasy? Do HBO's streaming numbers not rise? Do memorable children's novels not find second life as simplistic cultural mirrors?

"You see, *they* are Voldemort, and *we* are Emma Watson's Hermione, and if we find all these horcruxes—"

I'm ahead of myself.

Although MONBLACK's BAYWATCH would have suggested I was in significant danger, I felt fine stepping onto U.C. Berkeley's hilly campus. Indeed, the kids I saw all seemed like normal, quiet, going-about-their-business types, seemingly worried about standard student fare like doing homework and paying for textbooks and find-ing a job. (Some also seemed worried about what at one point would have been called "chasing tail" or "getting it in," but you could tell they wouldn't have liked such terminology unless it were used in an ironic, sex-positive way. The current term of art, after all, was "signing consent forms together.")

When I showed students a photo of Kevin, most shrugged and said sorry, it's a big school, you should try the quad, but a few went white and wide-eyed, running away while imploring me to do the same. Finally, I thought to add something about Harry Potter.

The student looked around to ensure nobody was listening. He leaned into my ear and whispered, "You can find him doing trials in Clark Kerr."

"Trials?"

"I can't say more. I shouldn't even be talking to you. *Damn you, Harry*," he said before running off.

As I searched for a campus directory that could guide me to Clark Kerr, I grew increasingly annoyed by the whole damned day.

You know, I thought, *maybe Trent was right. Maybe we should just give you what you wanted. Do nothing but appeal to your basest inclinations. It would be a hell of a lot simpler than this tedium, and anyway, who was I to judge? Was this not my longtime view — that our work should be accessible, our messages obvious — taken to the logical extreme? Where did art end and O-Bambi memes begin? Was this even a meaningful distinction anymore? Sure, maybe in the new dispensation a couple of PolitiFact reporters got zapped, but net-net, maybe that was fine? I mean, personal derangement didn't have to lead to social chaos, right? Right. Plus, personal derangement was something you were prone to anyway. If it weren't memes, it would be something else.*

Yeah, I thought, growing more confident, *maybe it was all fine. Maybe I'd been worried for nothing. Maybe I could go back to Nuevo...*

Then I saw the guillotine in the middle of the quad.

A large assembly stood in front of a stage, where Kevin paced between the guillotine and a group of tied-up college kids. He was yelling into his phone, prompting his supporters to yell into their phones.

"THIS IS GOING TO BE LIT AF, KEVIN," said one.

"ALL I WANT FOR CHRISTMAS IS A WHITE GENOCIDE," said another (who, confusingly enough for someone who hadn't attended an elite school and read the literature, was white).

However, behind their triumphant Mic.com calls I sensed a kind of cosmic disappointment. In recording their militant missives they tended toward mania, energetically checking their phones for any engagement and growing despondent when no engagement was forthcoming. (Of course, no engagement was forthcoming because all of their friends were in the same assembly yelling into their phones.) Some reacted by trying again and upping the ante (e.g., calling for a white *American* genocide, etc.), while others quietly took down their videos and scrolled through Reddit, depressed and digitally alone.

To cut through whatever you'd call this, Kevin needed to be sensational.

"THE FIVE YOU SEE BEFORE YOU," he said, sounding like someone who'd been banned from talk radio for going too hard, "STAND ACCUSED OF THAT MOST MISNAMED OF CRIMES: MICROAGGRESSION."

His intensity seemed to buoy the assembly's flagging spirits, so they yelled into their phones with renewed vigor. He continued, volume still at eleven: "WE WILL GIVE THEM A CHANCE TO EARN BACK THEIR ENLIGHTENED DESIGNATION..."

The assembly booed into their phones.

"...BUT ONLY IF THEY PASS THAT MOST SERIOUS OF TRIALS."

The assembly cheered into their phones.

"COME HERE, SAUNDRA."

One of the tied-up students got up from her chair. She stumbled across the stage and stood in front of Kevin, who'd prepared an iPad.

"SAUNDRA," he said, "YOU STAND ACCUSED OF ASKING A DINING HALL EMPLOYEE: 'So you think your daughter could get in here, then?'"

Saundra began bawling: "I know how it came out, but I was genuinely asking—"

"DON'T TELL IT TO ME, SAUNDRA."

"—I was going to help her with her application! I apologized to him immediately! He thought nothing of it!"

"TELL IT TO THE BUZZFEED 'HOW WOKE ARE YOU?' QUIZ."

Saundra's cries grew louder, but they were drowned in the sound of the assembly roaring into their phones.

Kevin held up his hands to signal quiet and began: "Question 1. Why is the movie *Boys Don't Cry* problematic?"

"Uh, could you use it in a sentence?"

"THIS ISN'T A SPELLING BEE, SAUNDRA. ANSWER THE QUESTION."

"I don't know — I've never seen the movie!"

"Allow me to refresh your memory: In the 1999 film, Hilary Swank plays female-born Teena Brandon, who adopts his male identity, Brandon Teena, and attempts to find himself and love in Nebraska before meeting a tragic end at the hands of a bigoted society."

"1999?! This movie came out like ten years before we were born. Why would this quiz even—?"

"Clock's ticking, Saundra…"

"I DON'T KNOW I'VE NEVER SEEN IT."

Kevin shook his head. "The answer, of course, is that no actual trans actors were cast in the movie."

"LIT LIT LIT," one of the assembly members yelled into his phone.

"Oh," said Saundra, "well…"

"YOU HAVE SOME REACTIONARY COMMENT TO MAKE, SAUNDRA?"

"No, no, I mean — that seems like a good point, actually. Although before jumping to conclusions, I do think it would be good to understand the moment in which the film came out. We should understand what it was hoping to accomplish and what it meant to people — including and especially trans people. Surely, we could consult the work of film scholars and put our discussion in the proper context, no? As it stands, this question removes all nuance, all context, and *that's* where we need to live, right? This seems like nothing more than an in-group/out-group sorting mechanism, in which the real and valid social critique is incidental to rewarding possessors of certain esoteric knowledge. But we should be inquisitive?"

This seemingly sensible perspective froze Kevin and his assembly. They coughed, shuffled their feet, and coughed again.

I could sense, for the first time since I'd landed on Earth, a creeping indecision, a lonely reckoning, a quiet moment. A moment in which information was processed, Bayesian priors updated, the ambiguity and complexity of life felt fully and profoundly. A moment in which one thought, *had* to think, "Maybe I don't know everything."

But then…

PING: "Russian Interference!"

PING: "Border wall!"

PING: "I'm no longer paying your tuition!"

Ping! Ping! Ping! Ping! Ping! Ping! Ping!

Phones were removed…

Things were read…

Thoughts were short-circuited…

And, thus, the moment was gone.

"LIT LIT LIT."

"LIT LIT LIT."

"LIT LIT LIT."

Hoping to seize the LIT moment, Kevin began reading Question 2, but the fervor of the assembled had grown too intense to be sated merely by asking more questions from BuzzFeed.com.

"END THIS NOW," one of the assembly members yelled into his phone.

Another, also yelling into his phone, said, "JUST DO IT, KEV. SHE WILL NEVER PASS. SHE GOT A SCORE OF 'PUMPKIN SPICE LATTE' ON HER BUZZFEED 'HOW PRIVILEGED ARE YOU?' QUIZ!"

"I HEARD HER SCORE WAS 'DRACO MALFOY OF

HOUSE SLYTHERIN,'" someone else yelled into the same phone.

Kevin looked down at his phone to see his comrade's messages streaming in. Looking up, he said, "I don't know…"

The assembly held their breath. Luckily for them, Kevin was just now finding out that he'd need to pay his own way through college and thus could not afford to sacrifice engagement.

"…IF I WOULD BE HAPPY WITH JUST THE GUILLOTINE. GRAB ME MY AXE AND FAUX DIRE WOLF PELT."

The assembly roared, rewarding Kevin with a storm of hearts, likes, and cryptocurrency. Two members of the crowd brought him his axe and dire wolf pelt, while another grabbed Saundra and pressed her neck against a headsman's stone. Kevin, feeding off his earlier energy, walked toward Saundra while swinging his axe from left to right.

Saundra, who was being pinned by some guy in a Calvin Klein "WOMEN ARE THE FUTURE" T-Shirt, pleaded with Kevin between sobs, but she was drowned out…

A hundred Instagrams being opened…

A hundred personal commentaries being yelled…

A hundred people who, if they were being honest with themselves, would admit they were like 50% paying attention.

"You, Saundra," said Kevin, "have been deemed incapable of redemption by a mob of your peers."

The crowd, trying super hard to be "Present" but consumed by some things they'd found on Instagram while recording their Stories, gave a dull shout.

This prompted Kevin, who could see he was losing his audience but could no longer afford the financial hit, to say: "FLIP HER OVER, MORRY, WE'RE GOING TO LOB OFF HER LEGS FIRST AND WORK OUR WAY UP."

Holy shit, I thought, as the crowd — now back in — chanted, "LOB! THEM! OFF! LOB! THEM! OFF!"

"Why are you doing this?" I yelled. "It doesn't make any sense. It sounds like she basically agrees with you."

"This is *politics*, moron," he yelled.

I jumped onto the stage, but before I could grab him, a new member of the proceedings emerged, causing a stillness to sweep through the crowd. The interloper wore Adidas slips, an Alpha Phi Tank Top memorializing Alpha Phi's "PIMPS 'n' HOES" date party, and a Native American headdress. He gave me a thumbs-up and ambled to the lip of the stage, where he put up his hands and asked for quiet.

"G. dammit, Rob," said Kevin, "could you annoy us later? We're busy."

"I'm annoying you now," said Rob.

Kevin, sensing his supporters had grown intrigued by the arrival of an enemy, acquiesced: "Fine, what is it?"

"Oh, nothing, nothing… I just thought you'd want to hear my new rap-rock mixtape. It's called *DOWN WITH THE THICCNESS* and it has a bunch of jams: 'First Day Out (My Goldman Sachs Summer Internship),' 'Q State of Mind,' and my personal fave, 'WOK IT OUT.'"

Trying to pair his iPhone with a volunteer's wireless speaker failed a few times, but eventually, Rob's song — an uncreative remix to Unk's 2006 hit "Walk It Out" (which featured prominently in the 2007 dance film *Stomp the Yard*) — began:

NOW WOK IT OUT (Now wok it out)
NOW WOK IT OUT (Now wok it out)
NOW WOK IT OUT (Now wok it out)
NOW WOK IT OUT (Now wok it out)

GUANGDONG WOK IT OUT
HUNAN WOK IT OUT
JIANGXI WOK IT OUT
SHANDONG WOK IT OUT
NOW HERE WE GO

The assembly flipped their shit.

"Appropriation!" one yelled into his phone.

"Offensive!" one yelled into her watch.

"The wok isn't even used in Shandong cuisine!" one yelled into her iPad.

And so it went: Angry shouts. Angry tweets. Angry Medium posts. Reluctant downloads. In the confusion, Saundra slipped away, saying, "Thank you, Rob, thank you."

Rob winked again, and — seeming content with how his mixtape debut was going — sat down in the cross-legged pose of the Buddha, awaiting the mob's vengeance.

"Rob," said Kevin, trying to ride the exploding powderkeg, "your album is not only problematic, but also *violent* toward every marginalized group on campus."

"I mean, not Mexicans," Rob offered.

"Intersectionality!" a member of the crowd yelled into her phone.

"Sure, then, I guess Mexicans," Rob agreed.

"GET HIM, EVERYONE!" said Kevin.

The mob stormed the stage and pulled Rob into the swarm. As they did, sending up eyeballs, fingers, fecal-spewing intestines, I thought of a few things: (1) I should have called the cops way earlier; (2) It's possible meme-ery developed as a way of dealing with chaos, since a lot of kids were now streaming the proceedings while invoking the now-classic "That Escalated Quickly" meme featuring Will Ferrell; and (3) Why the hell had I been viewing Rob as some sympathetic, even heroic, figure? The only thing I despised more than parody rap remixes were ironic rap covers (especially when the only 'ironic' part of the cover was that the singer was white or earnest or a child). And not only had Rob recorded a parody rap remix, but he was dressed like a real asshole. I mean, a Native American headdress? The backlash to *Boys Don't Cry* may have been overwrought, but I thought we were well beyond the point of being offensive for its own sake.

That's when I realized: *I'd been plugged into Karen's emotional frequency this whole time. This was all happening in her imagination.* I did a few jumping jacks to reset my worldview and looked at the quad anew: The axe and dire wolf pelt were no longer there. Nor were the stage and guillotine. No classmates were being torn limb from limb, and no music was being played. There *did* seem to be a protest going on, and Kevin *did* seem to be leading, but it was far more innocuous than what Karen had been fearing.

A passing alumna in a "Berkeley Mom" Patagonia fleece-vest even remarked to her daughter, "Ah, I remember my days of protest… We used to care so much, you know? Do you want to go play protest, honey?"

"MOM. *LAME*," her daughter said.

"Just asking, just asking. You won't be able to do this once you graduate, you know. So, anyway, like I was saying: That new Dove shampoo Beyoncé? SOOO good. We're really *smashing the patriarchy*, wouldn't you say, sweetie?"

"UGH."

In an echo of my earlier hallucination, Saundra was being booed by her classmates.

"Surely, friends," she pleaded, "we should voice our opinion about *The Vagina Monologues*, and express unreservedly our wish for the Berkeley Theater Company to perform something other than *The Vagina Monologues*. But surely we can also agree that they can perform it if they want to. Threatening their show will only lead to a backlash among like-minded, convertible folks, and we should be focused on bringing them to our side, not on righteous indignation!"

"I'd like to have a monologue with *your* vagina!" Rob yelled.

For some reason, hearing Rob's provocation pulled me into his emotional orbit, causing my world to transform once again. But unlike Karen's emotional frequency, Rob's initially felt like nothing. It was static. White noise. His worldview seemed valueless beyond an obsession with dated jokes. But beneath that emptiness hid something sinister, which I felt growing stronger as I lingered in his headspace. This… *thing*, I guess you'd call it, was rage, yes, but it was rage tinged by fear. A siege mentality in which Kevin (despite being, you know, nineteen) drove the siege engine of intellectual oppression, an Orwellian Trebuchet that threatened everything Rob held dear: his Adidas slips, his rap career, his Goldman Sachs summer internship.

That's when I looked up and saw Rob's demons made flesh, carrying guns and beginning to surround the Clark Kerr quad. A mix of college students and lonely, middle-aged men, they called themselves "The Appropriators' Militia," and like Rob, they wore Adidas slips and Native American headdresses. However, to this basic ensemble many added Iron Crosses and Viking Ruins and honest-to-G. Swastikas. They addressed each other by military rank, a quirk so pathetic you almost wished you could feel bad for them…

"Blood and soil!" they yelled, cocking their guns. "Someone's gonna die today!"

For a moment, I thought this militia was maybe another hallucination — that I'd somehow slipped into Kevin's emotional frequency. But when I shut off my emotional radio and looked again, they were still there, borrowing liberally from the white supremacist's songbook.

Thus, I finally came to see what DeMar meant when he said I'd built a Tower of Babel:

BUT G. CAME DOWN TO SEE THE CITY AND THE TOWER WHICH THE SONS OF MEN HAD BUILT. AND G. SAID, "INDEED THE PEOPLE ARE ONE AND THEY ALL HAVE ONE LANGUAGE, AND THIS IS WHAT THEY BEGIN TO DO; NOW NOTHING THAT THEY PROPOSE TO DO WILL BE WITHHELD FROM THEM. COME, LET US GO DOWN AND THERE CONFUSE THEIR LANGUAGE, THAT THEY MAY NOT UNDERSTAND ONE ANOTHER'S SPEECH."

Which is to say: When your predecessors built a hubristic monument to their own genius, G. gave them a good Old Testament punking by scrambling their speech. And while the internet should have been your triumph — the tower to end all towers — I'd transformed it into a grandiose venue for disagreement, delusion, and misunderstanding. A place where any good-faith translative effort, any ruminative pause, would be beset by *PING* upon *PING* upon *PING* upon *PING* until only the simplest, purest, basest form of a statement could be transmitted, ensuring you had no space, no language, no volume to deal with the problems my tower had created.

And so, when it happened, it happened like a *ping* — familiar, natural, momentarily indistinguishable from an email promising you 50% off microfiber underwear (TODAY ONLY). *Is that blood...?* you ask, looking up from your phone. *Yes, yes, it's blood, but from where...? Streaming from someone's leg...? Ah, yes, Kevin's leg — Kevin is bleeding to death.*

One of the militia members has shot him, making good on their promise. Blood is pooling and people are screaming and sirens are blaring, and while I pray this is an emotional fantasy, I know it's real. I know it's happening. My dumb, desperate decision has led to a world that calls forth symbols — killer cops, kneeling football players, a dead college student — so that many sides — *MANY SIDES* — can momentarily occupy common ground, not so they can unite, but so they can talk *at* each other rather than merely *past* each other, so that whatever facts they share can be permanently and irrevocably split in two. Made binary like the machine code powering Nuevo's ever-rising revenues.

But in this instant, when Kevin is still dying and we leap immediately from tragedy to translating the tragedy in our own irreconcilable tongues, I am not thinking about any of this. I think only: *How will Karen see her grandson portrayed?*

At the risk of plagiarizing, I wept.

———————

The next day, classes were cancelled, and a memorial was set up for Kevin. If the memorial's attendees were looking for solace, they would be disappointed:

"THIS SHOULD BE CALLED WHAT IT IS," one of Kevin's friends yelled into his phone, "WHITE NATIONALIST TERRORISM."

"OR," Rob yelled into his phone in response, "MAYBE IT WAS COMEUPPANCE FOR A CARD-CARRYING MEMBER OF ANTIFA."

I zigzagged through the assembly until I was at the rim of the crowd. I looked around for someone to talk to, but everyone was busy arguing with their phones or trying to take a selfie with the memorial or recording YouTube videos about how Kevin's death had impacted them personally. I turned my head to avoid showing up in a student's selfie, and that's when I saw someone: a girl standing far away from the assembly, hands in her pockets, looking weary and sad. I walked up to her.

"Hey," I said.

"Hey," she said back.

"I'm Zeke."

"Zeke, huh?" She smiled. "Like 'Ezekiel,' the prophet?"

I laughed. "Yeah, kind of... but without the foresight."

We laughed together. After a few moments of silence, she said, "My name is Kamaiyah, by the way."

"Nice to meet you, Kamaiyah."

"Nice to meet you, too, Zeke."

"How are you feeling?"

"Pretty bad."

"Yeah — yeah, me, too."

"Did you know him?"

"Not well. We had a couple of classes together. He was always super nice one-on-one. I know he rubbed some people the wrong way, but this..."

"Yeah."

"I mean, the thing that bothers me — and I hope you don't think I'm insensitive for bringing this up now — is that I know this won't change anything."

"What do you mean?"

"Well, this *feels* like it should be a reckoning, you know? Like, at this point we have two options: We either call an armistice and sort out the extremely deep shit that led to this, or we don't, and destroy ourselves."

"Right."

"But I know what *will* happen is neither. We aren't going to choose. We'll just fight and argue and forget about it. And then we'll find something else to fight and argue and forget about. And we'll just keep doing that, again and again, ad infinitum. Modernity has become the ever-present sensation of passing gas."

I laughed.

She laughed.

I realized we'd been talking for a while without being interrupted, which made me think to ask, "Hey, do you have a phone by chance?"

She smiled and pulled out an old flip phone: "I broke my iPhone a few weeks ago. I was going to get it fixed, but then I started using this. I'll go back eventually, but for now, this is better."

"Really? It is?"

"Well, don't get me wrong — I miss some things. Like, I make music, so having Soundcloud on my phone was super convenient for responding to fans. Also, I was trying to meditate, and this app was helping me learn. But there was some junk on it, too, and I think if I had it right now, it would be hard to avoid being like… Well, like them," she said, pointing to the strung-out crowd.

"Huh," I said. "So you don't get, like, notifications on that thing?"

"Oh, God no," she said. "You can play Snake, though. Do you remember Snake…? That old arcade game?"

I was so taken with Kamaiyah, this person who seemed to be thriving in a world in which so few of you were, that I didn't notice anything unusual about her response, nor about the figure approaching from my periphery. Before I even had the chance to accidentally admit I inspired Snake back in the 70s, I was clocked on the head by a shoe.

163

SONS OF NOAH

I woke up in what seemed like a fruit canning facility, although my blurred vision, combined with my headache and the darkness of my surroundings, made me unsure.

"Welcome to our fruit canning facility," said a shadowy hooded figure.

"Yes… Welcome, *Zeke*," said a second.

"Uh, thanks," I said.

Moments passed, and while I couldn't see my captors' faces, I had the feeling they wanted me to continue. But what could I say? "So what kind of fruit do you can here?" seemed silly in light of the kidnapping, while "I can't believe you've managed to sustain a fruit canning business in the world's most expensive real estate market" could be seen as combative.

More moments passed.

While I couldn't be sure, I thought I felt disappointment emanate from my captors' hooded visages.

"YOU ARE WONDERING WHO WE ARE," one said in a deliberately leading way.

"Kinda," I said, "but I could use an Advil. You did some damage."

They shuffled their feet and coughed.

"So, uh, what kind of fruit do you can here?"

"WE HAVE NO TIME FOR IDLE CHITCHAT, ZEKE," he said before repeating, "YOU WISH TO KNOW HOW WE KNOW WHO YOU ARE."

"I assume you'll tell me given the theatrical vibe you've got going."

"Theatrical, Zeke? This is all too real… or do you need a reminder? Clock him again, Japheth!"

"I got him, Shem!"

"Wait, no!" I said, suddenly recalling my revelatory (albeit shoe-shortened) conversation with Kamaiyah. "Look — I'm sorry. I'm sorry. I'm remembering now. Remembering… everything. Please let me go! I need to find a way—"

"Need to find a way to *what*, Zeke?" the one named Shem asked. "To convince everyone to put their phones down for a day or two?"

"Not a chance," said Japheth.

"Wait… yes… How did you know?"

Shem scoffed. "Anyone who has spent even one damned second on this miserable planet — let alone driven on a freeway or been to a concert — would figure it out."

"Seriously, what an insight." Japheth rolled his eyes. "Gee, you know the thing *nobody* was doing twenty years ago but *everybody* is doing now? Could… could *that* have something to do with all of this?"

"Our point is: You are not so clever, *Zeke*."

The way Shem said *Zeke* gave me pause, so I finally gave in to his provocations: "Alright, fine, how do you know who I am? Why did you bring me here?"

"Ha!" said Shem. "In due time, *Zeke*, or should I say, 'Failed manager of the defunct and disgraced subsidiary that thoroughly failed in its mission to enlighten humanity, and indeed may have helped bring about precisely the opposite outcome.'"

"I mean, *super* clunky, but I guess the idea—"

"Shut up! You would do well to listen. There is much you don't know."

"Alright, then, fill me in. I'm not going anywhere."

"Dammit, we are *building* to that, Zeke."

"You do know," said Japheth, "that we've been repeatedly referring to you by your name to emphasize the information asymmetry between you and us, right?"

"I got that."

"G. dammit," said Shem. He held his hand up to his ear and appeared to address somebody who wasn't in the room: "He's not playing along, pop-pop."

Whoever Shem was speaking to, it didn't seem to be going well. At various points in the following forty seconds of silence, Shem looked angry, confused, disappointed. Finally, Shem whispered, "Okay, pop-pop…"

Shem turned back to me and said, "We have a message for you, *Zeke*… From pop-pop…. WE ARE THE SONS OF NOAH."

"Some people call us TSON!" said Japheth.

"Nobody calls us TSON," said Shem.

"They *would* if you didn't shut it down every time. It's called *branding*."

"Could you shut up? Let's get this bit over with."

"Fine: WE ARE THE 'SONS OF NOAH,'" jeered Japheth.

"But… Who *are* the Sons of Noah?" Shem asked.

Still glaring at Shem, Japheth continued: "We are Noah's descendants — and his descendants' descendants — and so on…"

"I'm Shem No. 99, for example."

"And I'm Japheth No. 101."

"And we are committed to fulfilling pop-pop's vision."

"Namely: To make everything in the Bible actually come true."

"Holy shit, this is still going on?" I asked.

"SHUT UP, ZEKE," said Shem. "This is important backstory. Where were we? Ah, yes. So… helping Esther foil Haman's plot?"

"That was us."

"Bringing David a couple hundred foreskins so he could impress King Saul?"

"Also us."

"Helping Daniel escape from the lions' den?"

"Us.

"Although it took a few Daniels."

"Honestly, I think the lions were just full by the end."

"Getting Lot drunk enough to sleep with his daughters?"

"Ugh… Us."

"To be honest, we felt conflicted about that one."

"Although what could we do?"

"The whole book is lousy with incest."

"Anyway, the point is: we've been successful, I think we can all agree."

The pair paused, looked at each other, and in a quiet, solemn way, continued, "But we've been stuck, Zeke. Stuck for eons. Stuck on…"

"Revelation."

"The Apocalypse."

"The End of Days."

I coughed: "Is this going to be a monologue? Because if so, I'm warning you — quota-wise — we've already had one—"

"SHUT UP, ZEKE, IT WILL BE WHAT WE NEED IT TO BE."

"So like we were saying," Shem said, "we've been stuck."

"STUCK!"

"For damn near one hundred—"

"HUNDRED!"

"—uh, generations."

"GENERATIONS!"

"Trapped—"

"TRAPPED!"

"—in the lion's den of plot points."

"PLOT POINTS."

Shem sighed and kept going: "Like a Sisyphus of Foreskin—"

"FORESKIN!"

"—each time we bring Saul his hundred foreskins—"

"FORESKINS!"

"—he demands one hundred—"

"HUNDRED!"

"—more."

"FORESKIN!"

Shem threw up his hands. "Alright, stop, stop, *stop*. What is this new thing you're doing?"

"I'm Migos-ing. People online like it. I'm *pushing* us."

"Well, stop it."

"STOP IT!"

"I'm G. damned serious. We're way behind as it is."

"Fine," said Japheth, who crossed his arms and looked away.

Continuing to eye his brother skeptically, Shem continued: "So like I've been *trying* to say, we've been stumped."

"And it's not for lack of trying," said Japheth.

"Indeed, we've had a number of promising opportunities—"

"—but bringing about the end of humanity is harder than you'd think."

"You know it, *hermano*. Remember when Rome finally fell?"

"Ah, what a moment."

"We were so naive then."

"Humanity's living standards *did* decline, but that only made them more religious and harder to talk to."

"Ugh, tell me about it."

"But when one door closes…"

"Another opens."

"Feudalism."

"Bingo, baby."

"When Feudalism happened, we figured, 'Hey, all we need to do is convince a few inbred lords and an already corrupt Papacy to turn on their people.'"

"And if we're being honest, we didn't need to do much convincing."

"Inquisitions. Crusades. The day-to-day drudgery of unremunerated farm labor."

"All things that — with time — would surely have broken

humanity's will to live."

"But then… *Gutenberg.*"

"GUTENBERG! Sorry, I wasn't Migos-ing again. Just angry."

"Don't worry, *hermano.* Let it out."

"That G. damned prick came along with his G. damned printing press and, suddenly, humanity was literate."

"Thinking for itself, even!"

"Try calling for a Crusade now!"

"Plus, the Plague, which we thought might bail us out—"

"Your jingle didn't do shit."

"—actually conspired against us."

"Yup, a bunch of peasants died, which only increased the bargaining power of the peasants who remained."

"Try making them work twenty-hour days *now.*"

"A massively unfortunate confluence of events, I think you would agree."

"And, so, ever since Gutenberg, we've been trying to drag humanity back to a pre-printing press world."

"We thought we needed to re-consolidate information into the hands of an authority."

"The Church. The Government. A Feudal Lord."

"So everything we built—"

"Newspaper monopolies. Radio. Film."

"—we hoped would have a consolidating influence."

"Would make it easier for a madman to assume the reins and drive humanity off a cliff."

"And while we had some minor successes here—"

"Stalin, for example."

"—consolidation wasn't all we thought it would be."

"Stalin isn't what you'd call 'scalable,' you know?"

"Plus, if you — G. forbid — ended up with a scruples-possessing asshole like Cronkite—"

"CRONKITE!"

"—then you're completely fucked."

"So consolidation: overrated."

"The Allied victory in World War II was a tough pill to swallow."

"But it *did* prompt an honest post-mortem."

"We finally realized we'd been like a French General at the beginning of World War I…"

"Dressing our soldiers in gaudy Napoleonic uniforms…"

"Sending our cavalry into a sea of machine gun fire…"

"You see, we'd missed some *major* things."

"The Thirty Years' War, for example."

"A big thing to miss, seeing as how eight million people died."

"And, more importantly, seeing as how it all began one hundred years earlier when Martin Luther used the printing press — what we thought was our mechanical enemy! — to publish anti-Papal broadsides."

"Knowledge—"

"Or some rough approximation thereof."

"—bred discontent."

"It also bred hysteria. Around the same time, you had humans going on massive witch hunts."

"50,000 women died for no reason."

"Humanity was literally just super freaked out about witches."

"And it became progressively more ridiculous from there."

"Yellow journalism."

"Charismatic Christianity."

"The Weathermen."

"Talk Radio."

"Modern finance."

"Cable News."

"CABLE NEWS!"

"Each a minor perturbation, each a sign our plan to re-consolidate wasn't as smart as we thought it was."

"You see, Zeke, we'd been trying to destroy the printing press when we should have been giving *everybody* a printing press."

"Sure, consolidation could land you a Stalinist radio address, but it could also land you an FDR fireside chat."

"*De*-consolidation, however…"

"Would land you innumerable Stalins."

"Innumerable Hitlers."

"Innumerable Mussolinis."

"And, surely, they would yell over any FDRs you happened to produce in the process."

"So that's what we — well, pop-pop — did."

I looked up, thinking I'd misheard.

"You heard correctly, Zeke."

"Your 'Trent' isn't some glorified IT guy."

"He's our Noah."

"And he's been building toward this for millennia."

"All he needed was for somebody to light the inspirational fuse."

"Which reminds me…"

"He had a message he wanted us to deliver…"

"Thanks, *jefe*."

I stared at Shem and Japheth, trying to process what they'd said.

"That was G. damned insane," I said, hoping they couldn't hear the doubt creep into my voice.

"Oh, really?"

"Yes, really. That was, by an impossibly wide margin, the most bananas thing I've ever heard."

Shem narrowed his eyes: "Have you ever thought, Zeke…"

Japheth continued: "…that *you* are the one grasping at bananas."

"You keep trying to enlighten humanity even though — deep down — you know they don't want enlightenment."

"They *do*," I said.

Shem and Japheth seemed taken aback, and to be honest, I was too. I continued, unsure of what I was saying until I said it:

"They *want* to do right. They do. I mean, sure, their aims are usually neutral: choosing the optimal fantasy football lineup, buying the right sweater for their dog, that kind of thing... But sometimes, uh, sometimes, their aims are good. *Noble*, even. They build things. They make music. They volunteer. They adopt. They, um... They, um... dress their dogs in sweaters when it's cold...?"

I paused and frowned, trying to figure out what I could be getting at. I continued:

"The problem is... We've removed nobility from the realm of the possible. Do you remember how... in the Tower of Babel... G. does more than confuse humanity's language... He also 'scatters them from there over the face of all the earth.' I always thought that was part of the punishment, but now, I think it was *mercy*. He knew... He knew that if he didn't do that, and humanity had to keep living together, side-by-side, speaking different languages, they'd go berserk. That's what's happening now, I think... They're looking for a way to live together... and failing.

"And I think — I really think — they *want* to find a way... but... they're drowning in information... overwhelmed by language... contending with perspectives they've never needed to acknowledge... The moment is complex... but the tools we've given them are so lacking... so incapable of *handling* that complexity... And coexisting *requires* complexity... Requires seeing somebody in 3D, not in 2D..."

I felt the room slipping out of my consciousness as my voice continued, seemingly on its own:

"You know, I always thought that if we made our work more explicit, if we *Crash*-ified our messages, we'd have more of an impact. But I see now that I was wrong. Without some nuance, some fuzziness, some *mystery*, people have nothing to grab onto: They're either 100% in or 100% out. Their cards are on the table, always, but instead of increasing understanding it only makes everyone realize how much they hate each other's cards. But that *can't* be how things work... It *needs* to be different... and... I just... if we could help them come together...? Develop some humility...? Maybe learn to see themselves in others...?"

I dropped my head, finally realizing I had no language for expressing what I needed to express. That the words I was grasping for were lost in the abyss of banality, of sentimentality, of cliché. That, indeed, my tower had been built atop this abyss, ensuring you — and me — would be unable to revisit our common knowledge even as the axioms upon which it had been built were destroyed. Like everything else, sentimentality had become fodder for ironic Instagram memes: *HAHAHA U MAD BRO? U MAD BRO? U MAD BRO? U MAD BRO?*

Yes.

I looked up, and as the room reconstituted itself in front of me, I saw Shem and Japheth smiling.

"I think we're ready," said Shem.

"Yup — I think we've talked enough," said Japheth.

Shem removed his phone from his pocket, opened his camera app, and said unto his followers: "YOOOOOOOOOO… What's going on, party people. We've got a jam-packed show for you today. It's going to be a big one. And for the PAAAAATRONS we've got some hot hot HOT content coming your way so if you haven't subscribed yet you need to SMASH. THAT. SUBSCRIBE BUTTON. And if you're not sure if you should subscribe, two things: FUCK YOU just kidding I love you, and here's a preview of that hot hot HOT premium content you're missing out on. DO IT, JAPHETH."

Japheth hit me with a shoe.

"Yes! There it *is*, *hermano*. And we've got way way WAY more where that came from, because — that's right, you guessed it — we're doing the first SHOE'ing in human history."

"It's like a stoning, but with shoes," said Japheth. "WE HAVE AN ASSORTMENT OF LEATHER-SOLED PROJECTILES AND THEY ARE READY TO STOMP THE YARD."

Shem shut off the phone and turned to his brother. "Quit making *Stomp the Yard* references," he said, "nobody remembers *Stomp the Yard*."

"We don't know that."

"We do. G. dammit, we do. Let's try this again." Shem re-opened his phone. "Sorry, patrons, technical difficulties."

"WE ABOUT TO HIT YOU WITH SOME QUICK PLUGS."

"If you become a Gold-level Patron, we will send you a *free* 'DEATH BY SHOE'ing commemorative T-shirt as part of your pledge."

"Remember — it's like a stoning, but with shoes."

"BUT TODAY — TODAY ONLY — IF YOU BECOME AN ARK OF THE COVENANT-LEVEL PATRON, WE WILL GIVE YOU THE COORDINATES TO OUR FRUIT CANNING FACILITY SO YOU CAN ACTUALLY TOSS A SHOE AT THIS GUY—"

"Whoa, that was fast!" said Shem. "We already have two upgrades. Come down to the coordinates we just sent and we'll get this fruit canning facility poppin'."

"JUST LIKE D.J. DID AT TRUTH UNIVERSITY IN *STOMP THE YARD*."

Shem groaned, grabbed the shoe from his brother's hand, and hit me in the head.

———

I heard some voices…

I opened my eyes…

In front of me, I saw two rotund twentysomethings wearing Crocs and Warhammer T-Shirts….

They held shoes above their heads.

"HE'S AWAKE," said Shem.

"IT'S TIME," said Japheth.

"FOR LEATHER-SOLED DESTRUCTION."

"WING-TIPPED BUGGERY."

"SQUARE-TOED ANNIHILATION."

"Get us started, Patrons."

The nerds, eyeing me smugly, held their shoes up higher, allowing the stench from their armpits to hit me in a preliminary strike.

Wincing and wishing I could plug my nose, I began to wish for a less preposterous demise. Why hadn't I simply found a job doing paperwork for Permits? Or spinning up routine Midwestern tornadoes for Natural Disasters? Why hadn't I found something simpler, easier, less futile? Becoming an Inspirer, I now realized, was the biggest mistake of my eternity. Bigger than *Pericles*. Bigger than my *Eye for an Eye* YouTube reboot. Bigger, even, than becoming a manager.

Okay, well, maybe not that big…

I sighed and braced for impact.

Moments passed.

More moments passed.

Even more moments passed.

"NOT COOL," said Shem.

"VERY *UN*-ARK OF THE COVENANT," said Japheth.

I opened my eyes to find that the Patrons had turned against their Patronees. Shem and Japheth huddled together, holding up their hands in an impotent defense.

"What do you want?" said Shem. "We can give you whatever you wa—"

One of the nerds struck him with his own shoe.

Japheth scrambled up a ladder to get away from the shoe-tossing assailants, but didn't make it far before being pegged by the other shoe.

He fell to the ground.

The Patrons high-fived, and as they turned, their beards and Warhammer gear melted away, revealing them to be Diana and Maribel. They ran over and untied me.

As they hugged me, I managed to say, "You… You came. I thought you'd abandoned me."

"What are you talking about?" asked Diana. "We told you we were going to find a way to shut all this down. Did you not hear us?"

"You *were* crying pretty loudly when we left you," said Maribel.

"But we assumed it was some bit you were doing to say you were sorry."

"I guess… I guess…" and then I realized it. I, too, had lost myself in the reality-distorting warpfield of Nuevo East. I had seen what I wanted to see, believed what I wanted to believe. I snapped out of it and said, "I have so much to tell you. Trent. The Sons of Noah. *THOROUGHGOOD*—"

"We know," said Diana. "They livestreamed all that. That's how we found you."

"We actually found out even more," said Maribel. "One thing you already know: Trent is Noah. But what you don't know is that he and G. had a thing, a romance. G. didn't want Noah to die, so he went *way* afield of *Standards & Practices* by making Noah an agent."

"Noah's been angling to end humanity ever since."

"Yup. At some point — right around the 2016 Republican Primary — G. realized what Noah was doing and confronted him. But Noah played G. perfectly by dangling the prospect of a romantic rekindling in front of him."

"Made up a story about how he felt weird 'sharing' G. with the rest of humanity and couldn't really *commit* until they were alone. Really weird shit," said Diana.

"Wow," I said, "how'd you figure all this out?"

"I wish I could tell you it was hard," said Maribel, "but it genuinely feels like no one is even trying to keep secrets anymore. When we left Nuevo East, we went to G.'s office to tell him what we'd seen. We were like three seconds into our description of the *NASTY GNATS* when he began bawling and explained everything."

"Honestly, in way more detail than we needed," said Diana.

"Favorite wine."

"Favorite song."

"Favorite position."

"And so on."

"G. damn," I said, "that's wild. So what's going on up there now?"

Diana and Maribel shared an anxious look.

"Well, G. disappeared after 'spilling the tea' — his expression — on him and Noah…"

"…but before he did, he put Noah in charge."

"So at our last Semi-Fiscal All Hands, we brought formal charges against Noah per *Standards & Practices 9.2.5*."

"But Noah just yelled 'FAKE NEWS FAKE NEWS FAKE NEWS.'"

"And then all of our colleagues hurled shoes at us."

"It was terrible."

"So, anyway, we came down here. We figured you'd be in trouble by now."

"Thank you," I said, unable to hold back a smile.

Then it was my turn. After I explained everything I'd seen — both real and unreal — since returning to Earth, Maribel looked at me with a determination I hadn't seen since the old days of *THOROUGHGOOD1*. "Time to end this," she said.

"But wait a minute," said Diana. "The old lady zapping the reporter. That *didn't* happen, right?"

"Oh, no, that was real."

"Jesus," she said.

"But I think I know what we need to do."

"We need to get everyone off their phones for a day or two, right?" said Diana.

"Wait, yes, how did you—"

"Honestly, anyone who's been here for even a few minutes could figure it out."

"Yeah, we actually came up with a plan," said Maribel.

"Whew, thank G. I've got nothing. What do we do?"

"Depends. How hard do you think it would be for us to impersonate these guys?" she said, motioning toward Shem and Japheth.

NO DATA

Within a few days, we were in Utah loading up a U-Haul with dynamite.

While a part of me felt wrong about harnessing the sad, sweaty delusions of TSON's patrons, I took comfort in the fact that the sooner our plan was complete, the sooner they'd snap out of their delirium and find something other than Henry Ford's *The International Jew* to obsess over. (Maybe anime.) As we drove down Interstate 15, Shem and Japheth's phone buzzed with updates.

From Virginia: "Approaching Amazon's Data Center. The world will finally know what it's like to have to shop at Walmart!"

From Oregon: "Taking a quick break from occupying the Malheur National Wildlife Refuge to blow up Google's Data Center. The world will finally know what it's like to have to search on Bing!"

From Shanghai: "腾讯？更像是zerocent!"

And so on.

I pressed harder on the accelerator, and the action began.

"Wendy's!" I said, "We should do Wendy's!"

"Not a chance. We're doing Carl's, Jr." said Diana. "It is by far their best dining establishment."

"It's so damned expensive. We might as well pick up a Michelin guide."

"Quit being dramatic!"

"Only if *you* quit being dramatic!"

"Look, look, look. How about a compromise?" said Maribel. "We'll go to Taco Bell."

Diana and I looked at Maribel aghast. We were gearing up to yell when suddenly — *whiz* — something burst through the driver side window and passed by our heads.

"Holy shit," said Diana. "Is someone shooting at us?"

I glanced at my side mirror to see an all black Toyota Camry pulling up alongside us. As it glided into my blind spot, I felt it ram into our rear left tire bank. When this failed to slow us down — *U-Haul: Solid as a Rock* — the Camry's passenger rolled down his window, stuck out a Tommy gun, and pulled the trigger. The rat-a-tat sound was so loud it felt like it was coming from inside our U-Haul.

"G. dammit," I said, "we should've taken a plane."

"THE PARALLELS WOULD HAVE BEEN DELICIOUSLY AND DARKLY IRONIC," said Brucie, who, I should have mentioned, had parachuted into the U-Haul rental lot to join us without explanation.

I sped up and swerved through traffic, causing the U-Haul to wail and groan as we dodged the Tommy gun's bullets. Diana managed a glimpse of our assailants.

"Noah!" she said, "and by process of elimination, his son Ham must be shooting!"

(It has to be said: Ham was — by a wide margin — the least accomplished of Noah's three sons. He was the unattractive Hemsworth. The Manning who didn't play football. The Ball brother who shoplifted. In Genesis 9:26, Noah had even put a curse on Ham, which may be why he was having so much trouble hitting the broadside of our 26-foot U-Haul now, although between our swerving and his erratic firing, the occasional deeply confused civilian was hurt, hit, or forced off the road.)

Noah pulled up alongside us and commanded Ham to shoot, shoot now, but Ham was reloading the Tommy gun. I slammed the accelerator to get out of shooting range, but it was futile: the U-Haul topped out at 55 miles per hour. Brucie said, "Godspeed, friends," and climbed out of the U-Haul through the sunroof. Diana, Maribel, and I looked at each other in confusion as Brucie's steps, sounding like hail against a tin roof, shook the cabin. Brucie yelled, "When you accept my National Book Award for Nonfiction, tell those fucking morons that there was no metaphor, no allegory, no fucking point. The whole thing was about trees."

In an unnecessary act of heroism, Brucie jumped from the U-Haul to the Camry, breaking himself against the Camry's windshield and forcing Noah and Ham off the road. Seconds later, we heard the blast of the Tommy gun and a leafy groan.

"Brucie!" I yelled. "Should we go back?"

"No time," said Diana. "We're almost there."

Facebook's Data Center came into view. We looked at each other and prayed. "For Brucie," I said.

"For Brucie," they said.

Almost there…

Almost there…

Almost there…

I held my breath, counted down from three, and yelled "OUT."

We tucked-and-rolled from the U-Haul and our vehicle ploughed into the data center, revealing a room filled with rows and rows of servers. A blue-and-white sign hung over the scene: "FACEBOOK MESSENGER," it read. The U-Haul exploded, beginning a domino-like sequence of fireballs that annihilated each building of the data center with a thundering commencement: *Boom!* Facebook Messenger. *Boom!* Newsfeed. *Boom!* Instagram. *Boom!* A massive building marked "TOTALLY ABOVE-BOARD DATA COLLECTION APPARATUSES." Employees rushed from the wreckage and sprinted to their cars in panicked zigzags, dodging the flames flying from their former office. One was hit in the head by a piece of U-Haul that broke down U-Haul's pricing options: $19.95/day for a 10' truck; $29.95/day for a 15' truck; and so on. He picked it up, stared at it, and looked back at his former office like a man overcome by the eminent fairness of U-Haul's pricing.

A smaller explosion was happening on Shem and Japheth's phone, as celebratory pings came streaming in from across the world. "Goodbye, Google!" "Hasta la vista, Amazon!" "Toodle-oo, Tencent!" TSON's patrons finally had a moment in their lives worth cheering, but the celebration wouldn't last long: As the final building in Facebook's Data Center tumbled inward, Facebook Live went black, and we were alone.

We opened Twitter: "No data."

Gmail: "No data."

Amazon: "No data."

Finally, the phone said, "No signal found. Please try again in a few minutes."

In the distance, we could hear Noah yelling and slamming his hands on the steering wheel. We continued to cheer and high-five, and even began to speculate about how quickly humanity's behavior would improve.

But that's when we felt it... Something terrible had been loosed... Some malevolent energy was breaking its chains and emerging from a place we couldn't name...

It was the creeping malaise, the horrifying darkness, the infinite gaping void.

It was the void you'd been avoiding by commenting on photos and extending Snap Streaks and retweeting hot takedowns. The void you'd been hiding from in niche listicles and even more niche memes. The void you'd been pretending to fill by being angry, knowing your anger had no real ambition, no genuine aspiration for power or for change, that it was, at bottom, a digital signal you emitted automatically, impotently, so that in exchange for allowing yourself to be reduced to a perfect, stylized advertising target, you could get more anger-provoking content that would stave off the void for one more day.

Buried in a desert of digital noise, the void had grown massive, malignant, boundless. And now we'd dug it up, completely unprepared to face it. The void consumed not only our spirit, but humanity's spirit, enveloping all of us — all of *you* — in an emotional black hole, a gaping maw that felt fearsome and bitter and cold. All at once, we realized we were in pain — spiritual pain, psychic pain — and that we'd lost our only way to cope, causing someone, anyone, I'm not sure who, to yell "OH MY GOD OH MY GOD PLEASE TURN IT BACK ON."

As Diana, Maribel, and I shook with metaphysical sickness, Trent/ Noah pulled up in his damaged Camry and stepped out, cackling. He sauntered over to us and said, "You morons… You perfect fucking morons… This is *exactly* what I needed you to do! You've exposed humanity's rotting core!"

"Then why did you to try to stop us?" said Diana.

"Yeah — why involve us at all?" said Maribel.

"When I touch up the Book of Revelation," he said, "I'm going to explain that I tried desperately to stop you. I'm still earning mad speaking fees discussing my management philosophy in Silicon Valley and D.C., and destroying the technology I profess to love wouldn't exactly be 'on brand,' you know? You also have to admit there's something poetic about the fact that you chose to respond to this dilemma with an act of impotent, symbolic violence rather than inspiring something new."

Diana, Maribel, and I shared a pained look. Maribel staggered to her feet.

"G. is going to intervene," said Maribel. "He's going to stop this."

"*G.?*" Noah said, almost spitting out the name. "Don't you see? *G. is dead, muchachos.*"

"Wait a minute," I said, "is he really dead, or are you just quoting Nietzsche —"

"Albeit in the stupidest way possible," said Diana.

"The fact that you still think that's a meaningful question shows me you haven't learned a God. Damned. Thing."

Noah resumed laughing as we fell to the ground in anguish. I looked up to find motorists pulling over on the freeway to do the same. After millennia of trying, Noah had finally succeeded in making people as miserable as he was. He ran around us, hands over his head.

"Champiooooooon of the world!" he yelled, and even when the police arrived to start cordoning off the smoldering building he was engaged in what looked like a grotesque touchdown dance.

Smoking an e-pipe, a detective walked around us, occasionally crouching down to mumble "Hmm" or "Ahh" or to pass gas. Sometimes, he'd get on his stomach and crawl around like a worm, shouting "Yes! Yes! WARMER, Jerry," while at other times, he would shut his eyes and look to the sky like he was communing with a ghost. At one point, after he'd grown bored of showing us he could hop on one leg while chewing bubble gum, he pulled down his pants and began to sing Britney Spears' "Toxic."

"Can he not feel it?" I whispered.

"I think he's so far up his own ass he can't," said Diana.

He froze: "I'VE GOT IT. Ah, yes — yes, of course. It's all so simple. You see, my boy? The Black Camry? The guns? These two are clearly members of a Central American drug cartel."

"Ah, of course, it makes so much sens—" the cop beside him started.

"Were it only so simple, lad. See the robes? This is no regular Central American drug cartel. No, this drug cartel is backed by ISIS. An ISISian drug cartel harassing these kind, noble, all-American truck drivers." Turning to us, he asked, "What was in your truck, dears?"

"Uh, I think—"

"No need to answer, of course, we already know: Mattresses. Memory foam mattresses in which to transport all manner of important government weapons."

"Dude — this is Utah. I don't think an ISIS-backed—"

"Shut up, Diana," whispered Maribel.

"Yes — yes yes yes yes yes *yes*," he said, ignoring Diana and Maribel completely. "These religious fundamentalist cartel members—"

"Not the *good* kind of religious fundamentalist, either," the cop added.

"Yes. Not the good kind. They thought they could hijack your vehicle, steal America's weapons, and force Utah's teens to shoot heroin and have premarital sex. But you — *you* — you wouldn't submit so easily. YOU ARE HEROES," he said, tears suddenly in his eyes. Looking to the sky, he added, "The heart and soul of America, the truck driver is. Were I a better man, I would like to think *I* could have been a truck driver, but no, no, I'm a humble detective."

"But a damn goo—" the cop began to say.

"BUT A DAMN GOOD ONE," the detective interrupted. "I believe our work here is done, wouldn't you say, my boy?"

"Wow — what a master! Isn't he a master?" said the cop.

We simply stared.

The cop continued: "Well, let's book 'em, then, eh?"

"I would say so," said the detective. He took a long drag from his e-pipe.

The cop shoved Noah and Ham into the squad car. Ham, of course, was crying. But Noah looked happy — triumphant, even. He knew humanity would soon collapse into the void he'd fooled us into opening.

"This is what they get for leaving me out of their suicide pact!" Noah said. "Now *I'm* going to be the only one left alive."

As the chill consumed my body, I knew he was right. I had felt the world come apart. I could sense the despair as humanity impotently swiped their phones — hoping they would refresh, knowing they wouldn't. The online arguments about video games and net neutrality were about to spill into the real world in a way that would make what happened at Berkeley look innocuous.

PART 3:

The DMV

PASSWORD PRIMEVAL

Weeks had passed since we'd unleashed the creeping malaise/horrifying darkness/infinite gaping void, and while all systems were back online (the NSA, it turns out, backs up all of your data), the void remained, sanding down humanity's spirit in a slow, workmanlike way. Thus, you continued to mainline memes and passive-aggressively comment on photos of your friends' kids, but in a sad, impotent, excessive way — the way a Roman Senator would have partied in 244 AD, formal powers long gone, notional powers soon to follow: "hey wow she's so big now guess it's been a while since we've seen you lol but who cares lol." Your looming implosion, your consumption of yourselves, was by now inevitable: It might take weeks, months, or years, but Diocletian would pass his reforms, the Germanic tribes would crash through your gates, the void would pull you in.

But, for now, we had a Defensive Driving class to go to. Although the detective felt this mandate necessary ("Utah has become something of a nanny state," he explained), we'd also been hailed by the press, in a painful bit of sponsored content, as "The Affordable Bl-U-Haul Line" in the fight between Utah and ISIS, the point being: When we pulled our new U-Haul into the DMV, we hoped no one would scrutinize its mural (a mechanized Bald Eagle drone bombing a mosque).

We sat in the U-Haul for a few minutes in silence, pondering all that had happened. Finally, Maribel spoke. "I can't... I honestly can't believe it's come to this."

"Yeah..." sighed Diana.

"Centuries of work. Millennia of inspirations. Eons of trying to help human beings grow into better versions of themselves. All of it… All of it culminating in a trip to the Salt Lake City Department of Motor Vehicles."

"Should we, uh, go do something else?" I asked. "Technically, we don't need to drive."

Maribel ignored me. Diana touched Maribel's forearm. "The universe is a cruel place," said Diana.

Maribel looked down at the leaves and Arby's wrappers strewn about the U-Haul's cabin floor. For a moment, I could see tears filling her eyes. She turned to the door and said, "Well, we've thoroughly bungled *THOROUGHGOOD1*. Humanity will need to work out *THOROUGHGOOD2* for themselves. May God help them, wherever he is."

Walking in, we found the familiar scene we'd parodied in our work so many times before: confused people doing the Obsequious Lean while saying something like "Hello there — oh, my, what a lovely blouse — would you happen to know where I could find this room?"; jaded DMV employees answering by flipping through airline magazines (the only thing they kept from their trips to Cancun). Of course, given the creeping malaise/horrifying darkness/infinite gaping void, the proceedings were shrouded by a sinister pall: customers had an edge to their seemingly polite queries; DMV employees had swapped *Inflight Magazine* for library copies of *Moby Dick*.

Two complete flips through *Moby Dick* later, our number was finally called. Walking to the desk and Leaning Over Obsequiously, Maribel said, "Hello there — oh, my, what a lovely blouse — would you happen to know where we could find this room?"

Flip.

Flip.

Flip.

"That your U-Haul?"

"Yes."

"You don't find that painting on the side a bit ridiculous?"

———————

Passing through corridor upon corridor of linoleum, we grew weaker, although I couldn't explain why: The beige floor may have been reminding us of our harrowing trek through Nuevo East; the void may have been growing stronger and more punishing; the lighting may simply have been a tad unpleasant. In the doorway of Room 109A stood a portly gray-haired man, waving us in.

"Come inside," he said, "we are so, so happy you're here. Come, now, come in and have a seat."

The chairs in the room were arranged in a circle, and all but four were occupied. Diana, Maribel, and I took the three nearest the door, while the portly gray-haired man — our teacher, presumably — took the chair at the opposite end.

I looked around the room and took an account of some of my classmates: On my left, an annoyed-looking man in a Merino wool zip-up spun the keys to a Tesla around his index finger; next to him, a woman was anxiously shushing her kid, who seemed to be angling for a game of peek-a-boo; across from me, a college kid was scrolling through his phone, occasionally pausing to record thoughts for his YouTube channel "Sheeplopolis," while next to him, a woman with a professorial air was typing on a laptop; on the other side of her, a young woman was scrolling through her phone while a man in a "Don't Be Evil" T-Shirt insisted she try on his virtual reality glasses, which looked similar to the ones the agents in Nuevo had been wearing.

"Wonderful," said our teacher, "it's so wonderful we're all here, all together. Wouldn't you agree?"

No response.

"My name is Eugene V.," he continued, "but you can call me Gene. I guess you could say I'll be *driving* us through today's curriculum."

No laughter.

"Alright," he went on happily, "one thing before we begin: I'm going to pass around a basket. Please put your phones, laptops, and VR glasses in it. Don't worry, don't worry — you'll get them back at the end of the day."

The room managed a surprisingly unified groan.

"Oh, come on, now. You'll all be fine. What we're learning today will be valuable. I need your complete attention."

The room didn't seem convinced, as the students continued to groan while they transferred phones from palms to basket. Some snuck one last peek at Twitter, Facebook, or work email before saying good-bye. Grabbing the now-brimming basket of phones, Gene walked to his desk and locked it in his top drawer.

Almost immediately, I could feel the room panic, choke, seize: It was going through withdrawals. All eyes were on the drawer, willing it open like an arena willing a game-tying three into the hoop, or — more precisely — like a megachurch willing a demon out of Carol's Weimaraner.

The void grew.

Gene, however, didn't seem to feel it (or care if he did). He was busy failing to pair his own phone with a Bluetooth speaker.

"Whoa — wait a minute," said College Kid, "why can *you* have your phone?"

"I'm not the one in class today, am I?" said Gene, winking and scrolling through his music. "And don't worry, Spencer, I'm not planning to be on my phone. I just found a new singer on Soundcloud who's going to help us de-stress."

A spectral, reverbed voice came from Gene's speaker, and I had to admit — it did have a soothing effect.

"Ah, there we go," Gene said as he sat back down. "Well, we should get going, shall we? Tell us, Spencer, how did you end up in Defensive Driving?"

Spencer, who'd been jonesing for his phone more than most, took Gene's question as an invitation to unload. Jumping atop his chair, he said, "SOME PRIVILEGED ASSHOLE IN A TESLA SUV CUT ME OFF."

Gene smiled. "Hmm. Interesting."

"'INTERESTING'?"

"Well, yes, I'd say so."

"HOW IS THAT 'INTERESTING'? HOW COULD THAT POSSIBLY BE 'INTERESTING'?"

"Well, are you positive he cut you off?"

"YES. I'M POSITIVE BECAUSE HE WAS AN ASSHOLE."

"Fine, fine, so he was an asshole. Let's move on. What did you do next?"

Spencer jumped up and down: "WHAT DID I DO? *WHAT DID I DO?* I DID THE ONLY THING I *COULD* HAVE DONE. I CUT *HIM* OFF AND SLAMMED ON MY BRAKES."

"Hmm."

"'HMM'-WHAT?"

"Well, do you really think that's all you could have done? Even if I accept your premise — he was an asshole — what did you accomplish by doing what you did?"

"HE WOULD HAVE KEPT DOING IT TO PEOPLE."

"So your retaliation stopped him, then?"

"Well…"

"Well, what?"

"I dunno."

"I think you do."

"Fine."

The moment lingered.

"Fine, what?"

"FINE, HE'S GOING TO KEEP DOING IT TO PEOPLE. I DID IT FOR MYSELF."

"Hmm, well, that's interesting too. So do you think he's more or less likely to cut someone off in the future?"

Spencer looked down. "More…"

"Yes! Good, Spencer! Good! Don't look so sad. That was brave of you to admit, and it brings us to Lesson No. 1 of Defensive Driving: You should allow the *vast* majority of shit to pass. Freeways are a septic tank, and if you allow yourself to become angry at every free-floating turd, you're going to be a completely ineffectual driver."

"But people are such *pricks*."

"They are," Gene nodded. "But if it helps, think about all the reasons someone could be driving poorly: They could be new to Salt Lake City; they could have a sick child at home; they could be zoning out after a stressful day at work. You don't know — you can't know — and if you remind yourself of that, you'll be able to keep your focus on the *road*, not the pricks."

The room was mostly nodding, but Spencer still seemed skeptical: "So we just roll over, then?"

Gene shook his head: "No, not necessarily. What would have happened, Spencer, if you'd engaged this driver privately?"

Diana sat up in her chair. "Whoa," she said, "I don't think a defensive driving teacher should be telling us to *talk* to people who cut us off."

"Shut up, Diana," whispered Maribel.

Moments passed.

More moments passed.

Spencer's frown became a smile. "I dunno."

"Right, *you don't know*. All we do know is that you got somebody as angry as you were, and for a moment, that made you feel better. But it accomplished nothing."

"Yeah!" said Tesla Guy, and — in a weird non-sequitur — added: "You were just mad at him because he drove a Tesla."

Spencer's smile disappeared. "THAT'S A SIMPLIFICATION AND YOU KNOW IT."

"YOU LITTLE PRICK—"

"Whoa — whoa now," said Gene. "Now, Mark, it seems like you had a strong reaction to this discussion. Why's that?"

"Ever since I bought a Tesla, everyone thinks I'm a prick... but I'm a nice guy!"

"So you're responding to Spencer's first comment?"

"Yes."

"Hmm. Well, let's change it up, then — how did you end up in Defensive Driving?"

Now fuming, Mark stopped spinning his keys and — like Spencer — jumped on his chair. "I *SHOULDN'T* be here, but this *BITCH*," he said, pointing to the peek-a-boo dodger, "thought it would be *FUN* to go *FORTY* on the freeway, and—"

Gene jumped up and said, "Whoa, whoa, whoa. Hold on, Mark. I wasn't inviting you to lash out at Jenna here, and if you do that again, you'll need to leave — without your license, I might add. Jenna has nothing — *nothing* — to do with why you're here. The fact is: *You* were the one tailgating; *you* were the one who couldn't stop when someone — it doesn't matter who — had to stop themselves, right?"

"Maybe."

"Maybe?"

"Yes."

"And how did you react in that moment?"

"I can't remember."

"Did you react angrily? Like you did now?"

"I can't remember."

"Part of passing this class is being honest, Mark."

"I can't remember."

"Well, maybe we should ask Jenna, then."

"Fine, I might've."

"Might've what?"

"Yes."

"Yes what?"

"YES I REACTED ANGRILY."

"Yes — yes. *Good.* That was brave of you to admit, Mark. You blamed somebody else, which is always, always, *always* the most tempting thing to do. Look everyone," Gene added, suddenly somber, "I'm not going to lie to you: This class will be hard. But only because *defensive driving itself* is hard. And, look, I'm not dumb. I know you don't want to be here. I know before you got into your cars this morning, you told your friends, your roommates, your spouses: 'This is such a waste of time. I don't need this.' But I'm beseeching you: Suspend disbelief for a few hours and consider the following: Maybe you *do* need this.

"Think back — think back to that moment today when you got into your car: Do you even remember it? Were you even present for it? Don't worry, you can be honest. The answer is 'No.' Your mind was busy. Occupied by family problems. By work problems. By financial problems. And *these* problems, more than anything, are the precursors to undefensive driving.

"So, Lesson No. 2 is: You need to learn how to take care of yourselves. Defensive driving isn't some simple set of mechanical techniques. It's not a mere reminder to use your turn signal and wait a few moments before attempting a lane change. It's much more — a holistic approach to living your life. It's a reminder to sleep more: A lack of sleep is associated with undefensive driving, and yet, our culture seems to fetishize lack of sleep. It's a reminder to spend your time forming social bonds: People who spend more time with friends and family are much less prone to undefensive driving. It's a reminder to get your financial house in order: Financial stress is a primary cause of undefensive driving, and we can combat it with a behavioral playbook: automatic withdrawals, passive indexing, etc."

"Whoa, wait a minute, are you qualified—?"

Gene kept going: "And, I know — I know, I know — the economy hasn't been working for the average person for a long time now, but maybe this is a chance to form social bonds by making things happen *politically.* You see, defensive driving is *not* an individualistic pursuit. It's all prep work. Prep work which allows you — in that blood-boiling moment, when defensive driving seems like an impossibly tall order — to remember that the car next to you isn't a car, but a human being. Who's going through the same financial, work, and family problems."

Gene, who'd by now gone a bit afield of any DMV-approved curriculum, brought it back to something vaguely resembling a defensive driving class: "You see, Mark? I know why Jenna was driving slowly that day, but I don't think you do. And, I think, if you did, you wouldn't be so quick to blame her. Jenna?"

Jenna, appearing meek since Mark's earlier tirade, looked down at her lap: "I don't know if I want to," she said, "it's embarrassing."

"You can do it, Jenna," said Gene, "everything that happens in Defensive Driving stays in Defensive Driving."

Jenna took a deep breath.

"Okay," she said, "I had a boyfriend, and he… he wasn't the best. So I — I ended up calling the cops a lot, and then one day — the day Mark and I got into our accident — my landlord told me my rent was going to be $400 higher than normal. And I remember… I remember crying in my kitchen, because I didn't know what to do. I had no way of getting $400, and I felt like a failure."

Jenna covered her eyes with her hands.

The professorial woman (who, it turns out, was a professor) added: "God, that's such a bullshit policy."

"It's a policy?" asked Jenna.

"Yes. It allows police to pass on certain costs to landlords, including, for example, domestic disturbance calls. Landlords, in turn, are allowed to pass the bill onto their tenants, so in practice, it's a de facto eviction notice."

"Oh, damn," said Glasses Guy, "I have some *great* literature on this. It's called *Evicted: Poverty and Profit in the American*—"

He stopped when he saw the room glaring at him.

"I had no idea," said Jenna.

"Few people do," said the professor. "Although if they did, I think there would be more outrage. I'm sorry to say it, Jenna, but your story is far from the exception. The policy ends up hurting women disproportionately, since they have to decide: 'Do I want to stay with my abuser?' or 'Do I want to be homeless?'"

Jenna nodded.

"Jenna, I'm a professor, and this is in my research area. If you don't mind, we could go to my office after this. I can take down your story, and I can give you some resources—"

"NOT ENOUGH," yelled Spencer, "WHAT WE NEED FOR CHRISTMAS IS A WHITE GENOCIDE."

The professor coughed. The rest of us stared blankly, fearful and confused.

Spencer coughed. "Uh, sorry," he said, "it plays on Twitter. What I mean is: I would be interested in organizing to fight this policy."

Gene jumped up: "Yes. *Yes.* I don't want to simplify this in some crude, make-believe way. I don't want to imply that so long as we get in a room and *Empathize*, things will be fine. The fact is: There are actual assholes. There are actual systems of oppression. And these smelly, oppressive systems prevent your fellow drivers from leading emotionally, spiritually, and economically complete lives."

"Um, so would you say this is still about defensive driving, or…?"

"It's all *connected,* Zeke, can't you see? So long as these systems exist, how can we expect our fellow drivers to drive defensively? We can't — or shouldn't — but we do: We do and it's not fair. And so we end up blaming one another for the sorry condition of our roads when in reality our roads are potholed and crumbling because we've stopped *investing* in them."

"Okay, so this *isn't* about defensive driving."

"It is, Zeke, it is. The great, galvanizing project of our time could be — *should* be — improving our goddamned roads. But in our sad, complacent, preoccupied state, it's become blaming *other* people for ruining *our* roads. It's tragically ironic: In a sea of information, equipped with the most powerful GPS humanity has ever possessed… When we could keep the keepers of our roads accountable like never before… could demand *better* like never before… We've simply allowed our freeways to degenerate into bumper cars.

"And when freeways become bumper cars, the only people who benefit are the ones who don't need to worry: It's the people who can drive on private roads, or the people who own the biggest bumper cars. *The people who win are those who are already winning.*

"The rest of us, meanwhile, end up bumping each other alive. And as we bump and get bumped, we become less understanding, and more paranoid, and quicker to anger. We become myopic. We forget we're driving on a freeway — *our* freeway. But if we're to survive, we need to remember the freeway is ours — *we* set the rules. *We* can choose to build empathy. *We* can choose to bump problems instead of people. *We* can choose to defend our fellow drivers without organizing frivolous bumping campaigns against every minor asshole. Even if we're forced to *drive* bumper cars, we don't need to fucking *use* them all the time."

Moments passed.

More moments passed.

The void was in a temporary stasis, not growing and not shrinking, making me think maybe — *maybe* — there was something here, that in a world where all of you seemed to be Driving Past Each Other or Talking Past Each Other, Gene had built an oasis, a path forward, a place where you could hear and be heard. Sure, he was overly earnest, and, sure, we were here under direct court order, but maybe — *maybe* — that was part of the magic? Tesla Guy *had* to talk to College Kid, and in so doing, they became not Tesla Guy and College Kid, but Mark and Spencer. For a minute, I thought I could feel the creeping malaise receding, sense the horrifying darkness growing less scary, feel the void shrinking, collapsing, could feel it being plugged by something indescribably pure: the energy you feel watching a close Game 7, surrounded by friends; the pulse you feel dancing at a wedding, surrounded by love; the cosmic reverberation you experienced when — once upon a time — you went to church.

But all of this was a glimpse, an impossibility, an illusion replaced immediately by something real. Mark stood up. He frowned and looked at Jenna. Kept looking at Jenna. He yanked at the Tesla lanyard around his neck as he opened and closed his mouth. In his mind, I could see him thinking back to couples' therapy, pondering all the billable hours he'd lost then and all the billable hours he was losing now, and I could see any semblance of sympathy he'd been feeling begin to tumble into the abyss of selfish consideration.

He turned around to face us and said, "So *this* is why I'm here? *THIS?* All of you are saps. MAYBE IF SHE HADN'T DATED SUCH A DOUCHE BAG, SHE WOULD HAVE NOTHING TO COMPLAIN ABOUT."

"Now, Mark —"

"I SHOULD BE EXEMPTED FROM THIS GODDAMNED CLASS."

The room reflected on Mark's words in silence. The sentiment he'd expressed was distressing, and — in a perfect world — they knew they would force him to apologize. However, they also sensed a promise in his words — or, more precisely, a way out of a minor inconvenience. Suddenly, idiosyncratic fears, worries, and concerns erupted, causing the floodgates to open as my fellow students grappled to explain all at once why they, too, should be exempted from this goddamned class.

One woman had been speeding on her way to work, worried if she showed up late again it would be the end. Others had been confused by nonstandard traffic controls, unfamiliar roundabouts, or massive four-way intersections that needed stop lights instead of stop signs. Some were here because they'd been arguing with spouses, kids, parents. Some were here because they'd moved recently and felt lonely. Some were here because they'd been passed over for promotion and had come to realize they'd never be able to afford that house, while others couldn't even think about a house, since they worked jobs they despised for people they despised but felt completely trapped — they were on their sixth semester of community college, doing everything people told them they should be doing, but they couldn't help but feel shysted, couldn't help but feel that the seventh semester of community college *wouldn't* be the one to unlock boundless opportunity.

And then the reasons grew personal and angry, as the students — sensing the void going supernova — fought for status, fought to be the last ones pulled in.

"WHY SHOULD A REACTIONARY PIECE OF SHIT LIKE HIM BE EXEMPTED?"

"Now, now, no one is going to be exempted—"

"MAYBE IF YOU'D WORKED HARDER INSTEAD OF SPENDING ALL YOUR TIME ON YOUTUBE YOU COULD HAVE A TESLA AND BE EXEMPTED, TOO."

"NO ONE IS GOING TO BE EXEMPTED—"

"YEAH, YOU KNOW, HE MAKES A GOOD POINT — WOMEN ALWAYS CHOOSE DOUCHE BAGS."

"NOW, STUDENTS, WE ARE LOSING THE PLOT—"

"IF I HAD TENURE I WOULD CLOCK BOTH OF YOU—"

"GREAT, SCORE ONE FOR THE OPPRESSIVE SYSTEM OF HIGHER ED—"

"THE THREE OF YOU."

"UTAH HAS BECOME SOMETHING OF A NANNY STATE," I found myself yelling, and was surprised to find Diana and Maribel joining in as well.

"THE HEART AND SOUL OF AMERICA."

"THE THIN BL-U-HAUL LINE."

As quickly as the room had coordinated, it now grew panicked and wild-eyed. The students swarmed Gene's desk and smashed it until it opened. They grabbed their phones and glasses from the ground and began to scream. Scream about the tyranny of the DMV. Scream about the privilege of Tesla drivers. Scream about the antagonism of college kids. They screamed about single mothers. About traffic control. About personal responsibility. The room screamed and screamed and screamed and screamed until all of the screams pooled into a single column of indistinguishable sound.

In the chaos, as our classmates were grabbing phones and glasses, the would-be peek-a-boo player pointed at the glasses on Glasses Guy and — in a stereotypically toddlerian way — said, "I want, I want," but Jenna had already snatched the glasses away and put them on herself. She dove into a virtual world — a world where only a single set of problems remained and she could ceaselessly rage against them. As she did, the creases on her forehead melted away, her eyelids drooped, her upturned lips waned to neutral.

In the real world, her problems would remain, but in her new world, progress.